This wa [D0777616] *normal.*

To be norma... ...to be able to walk into a room and not be concerned with what people thought they knew about her. Instead, Phillip had taken her at face value and made her feel welcome.

And he had a brother who was coming to dinner?

What did Matthew Beaumont look like? More to the point, what did he act like? Brothers could like a lot of the same things, right?

What if Matthew Beaumont looked at her like his brother did, without caring about her past?

What if he talked to her about horses instead of headlines?

What if— What if he wasn't involved with anyone?

Whitney didn't hook up. That part of her life was dead and buried. But...a little Christmas romance between the maid of honor and the best man wouldn't be such a bad thing, would it?

It could even be fun.

* * *

A Beaumont Christmas Wedding is part of
The Beaumont Heirs trilogy:
One Colorado family, limitless scandal!

* * *

If you're on Twitter,
tell us what you think of Harlequin Desire!
#harlequindesire

Dear Reader,

Welcome back to Colorado! The Beaumont Heirs are one of Denver's oldest, most preeminent families. The Beaumont Heirs are the children of Hardwick Beaumont, the third generation to run the Beaumont Brewery. The Beaumont Brewery is world famous for the team of Percherons that pulls the Beaumont wagon in commercials and parades.

Although he's been dead for almost a decade, Hardwick's womanizing ways—the four marriages and divorces, the ten children and uncounted illegitimate children—are still leaving ripples in the Beaumont family.

Matthew Beaumont is the third-oldest Beaumont Heir. But he wasn't always a Beaumont—not until his mother married his father when he was five. He was ignored by his father and overshadowed by his other siblings, so he tried his best to fit in. Somehow, Matthew became the one who "fixes" the scandals all the other Beaumonts leave in their wake.

Now Matthew is planning Jo and Phillip's wedding—it's the public relations event of the year! It's going perfectly, right up until a former child star named Whitney Maddox blows all of Matthew's perfectly laid plans apart. Will the maid of honor be a public relations nightmare and ruin the Beaumont Christmas Wedding? Will Matthew allow Whitney to get him off message?

A Beaumont Christmas Wedding is a sensual story about accepting your past and embracing the future. I hope you enjoy reading this book as much as I enjoyed writing it! For more information about the other Beaumont Heirs, be sure to stop by www.sarahmanderson.com!

Sarah

A BEAUMONT
CHRISTMAS WEDDING

—

SARAH M. ANDERSON

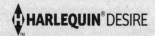

Recycling programs
for this product may
not exist in your area.

ISBN-13: 978-0-373-73351-4

A Beaumont Christmas Wedding

Printed in U.S.A.

www.Harlequin.com

SARAH M. ANDERSON

Award-winning author Sarah M. Anderson may live east of the Mississippi River, but her heart lies out West on the Great Plains. With a lifelong love of horses and two history teachers for parents, she had plenty of encouragement to learn everything she could about the tribes of the Great Plains.

When she started writing, it wasn't long before her characters found themselves out in South Dakota among the Lakota Sioux. She loves to put people from two different worlds into new situations and to see how their backgrounds and cultures take them someplace they never thought they'd go.

Sarah's book *A Man of Privilege* won the 2012 RT Reviewers' Choice Award for Best Harlequin Desire.

When not helping out at her son's school or walking her rescue dogs, Sarah spends her days having conversations with imaginary cowboys and American Indians, all of which is surprisingly well tolerated by her wonderful husband. Readers can find out more about Sarah's love of cowboys and Indians at www.sarahmanderson.com.

To Fiona Marsden, Kelli Bruns and Jenn Hoopes—
three of the nicest Twitter friends around.
Thanks, ladies! You guys rock!

One

Matthew Beaumont looked at his email in amazement. The sharks were circling. He'd known they would be, but still, the sheer volume of messages clamoring for more information was impressive. There were emails from *TMZ, Perez Hilton* and PageSix.com, all sent in the past twenty minutes.

They all wanted the same thing. Who on earth was Jo Spears, the lucky woman who was marrying into the Beaumont family and fortune? And why had playboy Phillip Beaumont, Matthew's brother, chosen her—a woman no one had ever heard of before—when he could have had his pick of supermodels and Hollywood starlets?

Matthew rubbed his temples. The truth was actually quite boring—Jo Spears was a horse trainer who'd spent the past ten years training some of the most expensive horses in the world. There wasn't much there that would satisfy the gossip sites.

But if the press dug deeper and made the connection between Jo Spears, horse trainer, and Joanna Spears, they might dig up the news reports about a drunk-driving accident a decade ago in which Joanna was the passenger—and the driver died. They might turn up a lot of people who'd partied with Joanna.

They might turn this wedding into a circus.

His email pinged. *Vanity Fair* had gotten back to him. He scanned the email. Excellent. They would send a photographer if he invited their reporter as a guest.

Matthew knew the only way to keep this Beaumont wedding—planned for Christmas Eve—from becoming a circus was to control the message. He had to fight fire with fire and if that meant embedding the press into the wedding itself, then so be it.

Yes, it was great that Phillip was getting married. For the first time in his life, Matthew was hopeful his brother was going to be all right. But for Matthew, this wedding meant so much more than just the bonds of holy matrimony for his closest brother.

This wedding was the PR opportunity of a lifetime. Matthew had to show the world that the Beaumont family wasn't falling apart or flaming out.

God knew there'd been enough rumors to that effect after Chadwick Beaumont had sold the Beaumont Brewery and married his secretary, which had been about the same time that Phillip had very publically fallen off the wagon and wound up in rehab. And that didn't even include what his stepmothers and half siblings were doing.

It had been common knowledge that the Beaumonts, once the preeminent family of Denver, had fallen so far down that they'd never get back up.

To hell with common knowledge.

This was Matthew's chance to prove himself—not just in the eyes of the press but in his family's eyes, too. He'd show them once and for all that he wasn't the illegitimate child who was too little, too late a Beaumont. He was one of them, and this was his chance to erase the unfortunate circumstances of his birth from everyone's mind.

A perfectly orchestrated wedding and reception would show the world that instead of crumbling, the Beaumonts were stronger than ever. And it was up to Matthew, the former vice president of Public Relations for the Beaumont Brewery and the current chief marketing officer of Percheron Drafts Beer, to make that happen.

Building buzz was what Matthew did best. He was the only one in the family who had the media contacts and the PR savvy to pull this off.

Control the press, control the world—that's how a Beaumont handles it.

Hardwick Beaumont's words came back to him. When Matthew had managed yet another scandal, his father had said that to him. It'd been one of the few times Hardwick had ever complimented his forgotten third son. One of the few times Hardwick had ever made Matthew feel as if he *was* a Beaumont, not the bastard he'd once been.

Controlling the press was something that Matthew had gotten exceptionally good at. And he wasn't about to drop the ball now. This wedding would prove not only that the Beaumonts still had a place in this world but that Matthew had a place in the family.

He could save the Beaumont reputation. He could save the Beaumonts. And in doing so, he could redeem himself.

He'd hired the best wedding planner in Denver. They'd booked the chapel on the Colorado Heights University campus and had invited two hundred guests to the wedding. The reception would be at the Mile High Station, with dinner for six hundred, and a team of Percherons would pull the happy couple in either a carriage or a sleigh, weather depending. They had the menu set, the cake ordered, the favors ready and the photographer on standby. Matthew had his family—all four of his father's ex-wives and all nine of his half brothers and sisters—promising to be on their best behavior.

The only thing he didn't have under his control was the bride and her maid of honor, a woman named Whitney Maddox.

Jo had said that Whitney was a horse breeder who lived

a quiet life in California, so Matthew didn't anticipate too much trouble from her. She was coming two weeks before the wedding and staying at the farm with Jo and Phillip. That way she could do all the maid-of-honor things—dress fittings and bachelorette parties, the lot of it. All of which had been preplanned by Matthew and the wedding planner, of course. There was no room for error.

The wedding had to be perfect. What mattered was showing the world that the Beaumonts were still a family. A *successful* family.

What mattered was Matthew proving that he was a legitimate Beaumont.

He opened a clean document and began to write his press release as if his livelihood depended on it.

Because it did.

Whitney pulled up in front of the building that looked as if it was three different houses stuck together. She would not be nervous about this—not about the two weeks away from her horses, about staying in a stranger's house for said two weeks or about the press that went with being in a Beaumont Christmas wedding. Especially that.

Of course, she knew who Phillip Beaumont was—didn't everyone? He was the handsome face of Beaumont Brewery—or had been, right up until his family had sold out. And Jo Spears was a dear friend—practically the best friend Whitney had. The only friend, really. Jo knew all about Whitney's past and just didn't care. And in exchange for that unconditional friendship, the least Whitney could do was suck it up and be Jo's maid of honor.

In the high-society wedding of the year. With hundreds of guests. And photographers. And the press. And…

Jo came out to greet her.

"You haven't changed a bit!" Whitney called as she shut her door. She shivered. December in Denver was an entirely different beast from December in California. "Except you're not wearing your hat!"

"I didn't wear the hat when we watched movies in your house, did I?" Jo wore a wide smile as she gave Whitney a brief hug. "How was the drive?"

"Long," Whitney admitted. "That's why I didn't bring anyone with me. I thought about bringing the horses, but it's just too cold up here for them to be in a trailer that long, and none of my dogs do well in the car."

She'd desperately wanted to bring Fifi, her retired greyhound, or Gater, the little mutt that was pug and…something. Those two were her indoor dogs, the ones that curled up next to her on the couch or on her lap and kept her company. But Fifi did not travel well and Gater didn't like to leave Fifi.

Animals didn't care who you were. They never read the headlines. It didn't matter to them if you'd accidentally flashed the paparazzi when you were nineteen or how many times you'd been arrested for driving while intoxicated. All that mattered to animals was that you fed them and rubbed their ears.

Besides, Whitney was on vacation. A vacation with a wedding in it, but still. She was going to see the sights in Denver and get her nails done and all sorts of fun things. It didn't seem fair to bring the dogs only to leave them in a bedroom most of the time.

Jo nodded as Whitney got her bags out of the truck. "Who's watching them?"

"Donald—you remember him, right? From the next ranch over?"

"The crusty old fart who doesn't watch TV?"

Jo and Whitney shared a look. In that moment, Whitney was glad she'd come. Jo understood her as no one else did.

Everyone else in the world thought Donald was borderline insane—a holdover hippie from the 1960s who'd done too much acid back in the day. He lived off the grid, talked about animals as if they were his brothers and discussed Mother Earth as if she were coming to dinner next week.

But that meant Donald wasn't tuned in to pop culture. Which also meant he didn't know who Whitney was—who she'd been. Donald just thought Whitney was the neighbor who really should install more solar panels on her barn roof. And if she had to occasionally listen to a lecture on composting toilets, well, that was a trade-off she was willing to make.

She was going to miss her animals, but knowing Donald, he was probably sitting on the ground in the paddock, telling her horses bedtime stories.

Besides, being part of her best friend's wedding was an opportunity even she couldn't pass up. "What's this I hear about you and Phillip Beaumont?"

Jo smiled. "Come on," she said, grabbing one of Whitney's bags. "Dinner will be in about an hour. I'll get you caught up."

She led Whitney inside. The whole house was festooned—there was no other word for it—with red bows and pine boughs. A massive tree, blinking with red-and-white lights, the biggest star Whitney had ever seen perched on top, stood in a bay window. The whole place had such a rustic Christmas charm that Whitney felt herself grinning. This would be a perfect way to spend Christmas, instead of watching *It's a Wonderful Life* on the couch at home.

A small brown animal with extremely long ears clomped up to her and sniffed. "Well, hello again, Betty," Whitney said as she crouched down onto her heels. "You remember me? You spent a few months sitting on my couch last winter."

The miniature donkey sniffed Whitney's hair and brayed before rubbing her head into Whitney's hands.

"If I recall correctly," Jo said, setting down Whitney's bag, "your pups didn't particularly care for a donkey in the house."

"Not particularly," Whitney agreed. Fifi hadn't minded

as long as Betty stayed off her bed, but Gater had taken it as a personal insult that Whitney had allowed a hoofed animal into the house. As far as Gater was concerned, hoofed animals belonged in the barn.

She stood. Betty leaned against her legs so that Whitney could stroke her long ears.

"You're not going to believe this," Jo said as she moved Whitney's other bag, "but Matthew wants her to walk down the aisle. He's rigged up a basket so she can carry the flower petals and it's got a pillow attached on top so she can carry the rings. The flower girl will walk beside her and throw the petals. He says it'll be an amazing visual."

Whitney blinked. "Wait—Matthew? I thought you were marrying Phillip?"

"She is." A blindingly handsome man strode into the room—tall and blond and instantly recognizable. "Hello," he said with a grin as he walked up to Whitney. He leaned forward, his eyes fastened on hers, and stuck out a hand. "I'm Phillip Beaumont."

The Phillip Beaumont. Having formerly been someone famous, Whitney was not prone to getting starstruck. But Phillip was looking at her so intently that for a moment, she forgot her own name.

"And you must be Whitney Maddox," he went on, effortlessly filling the silence. "Jo's told me about the months she spent with you last winter. She said you raise some of the most beautiful Trakehners she's ever worked with."

"Oh. Yes!" Whitney shook her head. Phillip was a famous horseman and her Trakehner horses were a remarkably safe subject. "Joy was mine—Pride and Joy."

"The stallion who took gold in the World Equestrian Games?" Phillip smiled down at her and she realized he still had her hand. "I don't have any Trakehners. Clearly that's something I need to rectify."

She looked at Jo, feeling helpless and more than a little

guilty that Jo's intended was making her blush. But Jo just laughed.

"Too much," Jo said to Phillip as she looped her arm through his. "Whitney's not used to that much charm." She looked at Whitney. "Sorry about that. Phillip, this is Whitney. Whitney, this is Phillip."

Whitney nodded, trying to remember the correct social interaction. "It's a pleasure. Congratulations on getting married."

Phillip grinned at her, but then he thankfully focused that full-wattage smile on Jo. "Thanks."

They stared at each other for a moment, the adoration obvious. Whitney looked away.

It'd been a long time since a man had looked at her like that. And, honestly, she couldn't be sure that Drako Evans had ever looked at her quite like that. Their short-lived engagement hadn't been about love. It had been about pissing off their parents. And it had worked. The headlines had been spectacular. Maybe that was why those headlines still haunted her.

As she rubbed Betty's ears, Whitney noticed the dinner table was set for four. For the first time since she'd arrived, she smelled food cooking. Lasagna and baking bread. Her stomach rumbled.

"So," Phillip said into the silence. His piercing blue eyes turned back to her. "Matthew will be here in about forty minutes for dinner."

Which did nothing to answer the question she'd asked Jo earlier. "Matthew is…who?"

This time, Phillip's grin was a little less charming, a little sharper. "Matthew Beaumont. My best man and younger brother."

Whitney blinked. "Oh?"

"He's organizing the wedding," Phillip went on as if that were no big deal.

"He's convinced that this is the PR event of the year," Jo said. "I told him I'd be happy getting married by a judge—"

"Or running off to Vegas," Phillip added, wrapping his arm around Jo's waist and pulling her into a tight embrace.

"But he insists this big wedding is the Beaumont way. And since I'm going to be a Beaumont now…" Jo sighed. "He's taken control of this and turned it into a spectacle."

Whitney stared at Jo and Phillip, unsure what to say. The Jo she knew wouldn't let anyone steamroll her into a grandiose wedding.

"But," Jo went on, softening into a smile that could almost be described as shy, "it's going to be amazing. The chapel is beautiful and we'll have a team of Percherons pulling a carriage from there to the reception. The photographer is experienced and the dress…" She got a dreamy look in her eyes. "Well, you'll see tomorrow. We have a dress fitting at ten."

"It sounds like it's going to be perfect," Whitney said. And she meant it—a Christmas Eve ceremony? Horse-drawn carriages? Gowns? It had all the trappings of a true storybook wedding.

"It better be." Phillip chuckled.

"Let me show you to your room," Jo said, grabbing a bag.

That sounded good to Whitney. She needed a moment to sort through everything. She lived a quiet life now, one where she didn't have to navigate family relations or PR events masquerading as weddings. As long as she didn't leave her ranch, all she worried about was catching Donald when he was on a soapbox.

Jo led her through the house, pointing out which parts were original, which wasn't much, and which parts had been added later, which was most of it. She showed Whitney the part that Phillip had added, the master suite with a hot tub on the deck.

Then the hall turned again and they were in a different part, built in the 1970s. This was the guest quarters, Jo told her. Whitney had a private bath and was far enough removed from the rest of the house that she wouldn't hear anything else.

Jo opened a door and flipped on the light. Whitney had half expected vintage '70s decor, but the room was done in cozy green-and-red plaids that made it look Christmassy. A bouquet of fresh pine and holly was arranged on the mantel over a small fireplace.

Jo walked over to it and flipped a switch. Flames jumped to life in the grate. "Phillip had automatic switches installed a few years ago," she explained. On the other side of the bed was a dresser. Jo said, "Extra blankets are in there. It's going to be a lot colder here than it is at your ranch."

"Good to know." Whitney set her bag down at the foot of the bed. The only other furniture in the room was a small table with an armchair next to it. The room looked like a great place to spend the winter. She felt herself relax a little bit. "So...you and Phillip?"

"Me and Phillip," Jo agreed, sounding as though she didn't quite believe it herself. "He's—well, you've seen him in action. He has a way of just looking at a woman that's... *suggestive.*"

"So I wasn't imagining that?"

Jo laughed. "Nope. That's just how he is."

This did nothing to explain how, exactly, Jo had wound up with Phillip. Of all the men in the world, Whitney would have put "playboy bachelor" pretty low on the list of possible husbands for Jo. But Whitney had no idea how to ask the question without it coming out wrong.

It could be that the Phillip in the kitchen wasn't the same as the Phillip in the headlines. Maybe things had been twisted and turned until nothing but the name was the same. More than anyone, Whitney knew how that worked.

"He has a horse," Jo explained, looking sheepish. "Sun—Kandar's Golden Sun."

Whitney goggled at her. "Wait—I've heard of that horse. Didn't he sell for seven million dollars?"

"Yup. And he was a hot mess at any price," she added with a chuckle. "Took me a week before he'd just stand still, you know?"

Whitney nodded, trying to picture a horse *that* screwed up. When Jo had come out to Whitney's ranch to deal with Sterling, the horse of hers that had developed an irrational fear of water, it'd taken her only a few hours in the paddock before the horse was rubbing his head against Jo. "A whole week?"

"Any other horse would have died of sheer exhaustion, but that's what makes Sun special. I can take you down to see him after dinner. He's an amazing stud—one to build a stable on."

"So the horse brought you together?"

Jo nodded. "I know Phillip's got a reputation—that's part of why Matthew insists we have this big wedding, to show the world that Phillip's making a commitment. But he's been sober for seven months now. We'll have a sober coach on hand at the reception." A hint of a blush crept over Jo's face. "If you'd like…"

Whitney nodded. She wasn't the only one who was having trouble voicing her concerns. "I don't think there's going to be a problem. I've been clean for almost eleven years." She swallowed. "Does Phillip know who I am?"

"Sure." Jo's eyebrow notched up in challenge. "You're Whitney Maddox, the well-known horse breeder."

"No, not that. I mean—well, you know what I mean."

"He knows," Jo said, giving Whitney the look that she'd seen Jo give Donald the hippie when he gave her a lecture on how she should switch to biodiesel. "But we understand that the past is just that—the past."

"Oh." Air rushed out of her so fast she actually sagged

in relief. "That's good. That's *great*. I just don't want to be a distraction—this is your big day."

"It won't be a problem," Jo said in a reassuring voice. "And you're right—the day will be very big!"

They laughed. It felt good to laugh with Jo again. She hadn't had to stay a whole two months with Whitney last year—Sterling hadn't been that difficult to handle—but the two of them had gotten along because they understood that the past was just that. So Jo had stayed through the slow part of the year and taught Whitney some of her training techniques. It'd been a good two months. For the first time in her adult life, Whitney hadn't felt quite so…alone.

And now she'd get that feeling again for two weeks.

"And you're happy?" That was the important question.

Jo's features softened. "I am. He's a good man who had an interesting life—to say the least. He's learned how to deal with his family with all that charm. He wasn't hitting on you—that's just how he copes with situations that make him nervous."

"Really? He must have an, um, unusual family."

Jo laughed again. "I'll just say this—they're a lot to handle, but on the whole, they're not bad people. Like Matthew. He can be a little controlling, but he really does want what's best for the family and for us." She stood. "I'll let you get freshened up. Matthew should be here in a few."

"Sounds good."

Jo shut the door on her way out, leaving Whitney alone with her thoughts. She was glad she'd come.

This was what she wanted—to feel normal. To *be* normal. To be able to walk into a room and not be concerned with what people thought they knew about her. Instead, to have people, like Phillip, take her at face value and make her feel welcome.

And he had a brother who was coming to dinner.

What did Matthew Beaumont look like? More to the

point, what did he act like? Brothers could like a lot of the same things, right?

What if Matthew Beaumont looked at her the way his brother did, without caring about who she'd been in the past? What if he talked to her about horses instead of headlines? What if—? What if he wasn't involved with anyone?

Whitney didn't hook up. That part of her life was dead and buried. But…a little Christmas romance between the maid of honor and the best man wouldn't be such a bad thing, would it? It could be fun.

She hurried to the bathroom, daring to hope that this Matthew Beaumont was single. He was coming to dinner tonight and it sounded as if he would be involved with a lot of the planned activities. She was here for two weeks. Perhaps the built-in time limit was a good thing. That way, if things didn't go well, she had an out—she could go home.

Although…it had been eleven years since she'd attempted anything involving the opposite sex. Making a pass at the best man might not be the smartest thing she could do.

She washed her face. A potential flirtation with Matthew Beaumont called for eyeliner, at the very least. Whitney made up her face and decided to put on a fresh top. She dug out the black silk before putting it aside. Jo was in jeans and flannel, after all. This was not a fancy dinner. Whitney decided to go with the red V-neck cashmere sweater—soft but not ostentatious. The kind of top that maybe a single, handsome man would accidentally brush with his fingers. Perfect.

Would Matthew be blond, like Phillip? Would he have the same smile, the same blue eyes? She was brushing out her short hair when, from deep inside the house, a bell chimed.

She slicked on a little lip gloss and headed out. She tried to retrace her steps, but she got confused. The house had a bunch of hallways that went in different directions. She tried one set of stairs but found a door that was locked at the bottom. That wasn't right—Jo hadn't led her through a door.

She backtracked, trying not to panic. Hopefully, everyone wasn't downstairs waiting on her.

She found another stairwell, but it didn't seem any more familiar than the first one had. It ended in a darkened room. Whitney decided to go back rather than stumble around in the dark. God, she shouldn't have spent so much time getting ready. She should have gone back down with Jo. Or gotten written directions. Getting lost was embarrassing.

She found her room again, which had to count for something. She went the opposite direction and was relieved when she passed the master suite. Finally. She picked up the pace. Maybe she wasn't too late.

She could hear voices now—Jo's and Phillip's and another voice, deep and strong. Matthew.

She hurried down the steps, then remembered she was trying to make a good impression. It wouldn't do to come rushing in like a tardy teenager. She needed to slow down to make a proper entrance.

She slammed on the brakes in the middle of a step near the bottom and stumbled. Hard. She tripped down the last two steps and all but fell into the living room. She was going down, damn it! She braced for the impact.

It didn't come. Instead of hitting the floor or running into a piece of furniture, she fell into a pair of strong arms and against a firm, warm chest.

"Oof," the voice that went with that chest said.

Whitney looked up into a pair of eyes that were a deep blue. He smiled down at her and this time, she didn't feel as if she were going to forget her own name. She felt as if she'd never forget this moment.

"I've got you."

Not blond, she realized. Auburn hair. A deep red that seemed just right on him. And he did have her. His arms were around her waist and he was lifting her up. She felt secure. The feeling was *wonderful.*

Then, without warning, everything changed. His warm smile froze as his eyes went hard. The strong arms became iron bars around her and the next thing she knew, she was being pushed not up but away.

Matthew Beaumont set her back on her feet and stepped clear of her. With a glare that could only be described as ferocious, he turned to Phillip and Jo.

"What," he said in the meanest voice Whitney had heard in a long time, "is Whitney Wildz doing here?"

Two

Matthew waited for an answer. It'd better be a damn good one, too. What possible explanation could there be for former teen star Whitney Wildz to be in Phillip's house?

"Matthew," Jo said in an icy tone, "I'd like you to meet my maid of honor, Whitney Maddox."

"Try to stop being an ass," Phillip said under his breath.

"Whitney," Jo went on, as if Phillip hadn't spoke, "this is Matthew Beaumont, Phillip's brother and best man."

"Maddox?" He turned back to the woman who looked as though she'd been stepped on by a Percheron. At least they could all agree her first name was Whitney. Maybe there was a mistake? But no. There was no missing that white streak in her hair or those huge pale eyes set against her alabaster skin. "You're Whitney Wildz. I'd recognize you anywhere."

Her eyes closed and her head jerked to the side as if he'd slapped her.

Someone grabbed him. "Try *harder*," Phillip growled in his ear. Then, louder, Phillip said, "Dinner's ready. Whitney, is iced tea all right?"

Whitney Wildz—Matthew had no doubt that was who she was—opened her eyes. A wave of pain washed over him when she looked up at him. Then she drew herself up.

"Thank you," she said in that breathy way of hers. Then she stepped around him.

Memories came back to him. He'd watched her show, *Growing Up Wildz*, all the time with his younger siblings Frances and Byron. Because Matthew was a good brother— the best—he'd watched it with them. He'd even scored VIP tickets to the *Growing Up Wildz* concert tour when it came through Denver and taken the twins, since their father couldn't be bothered to remember that it was their fifteenth birthday. Matthew was a good brother just taking care of his siblings. That was what he told everyone else.

But that wasn't, strictly, the truth.

He'd watched it for Whitney.

And now Whitney was here.

This was *bad*. This was quite possibly the worst thing that could have happened to this wedding—to him. It would have been easier if Phillip were screwing her. That sort of thing was easy to hush up—God knew Matthew had enough practice covering for his father's indiscretions.

But to have Whitney Wildz herself standing up at the altar, in front of the press and the photographers—not to mention the guests?

He tried to remember the last time she'd been in the news. She'd stumbled her way up on stage and then tripped into the podium, knocking it off the dais and into a table. The debate hadn't been about *if* she'd been on something, just *what*—drugs? Alcohol? Both?

And then tonight she'd basically fallen down the stairs and into his arms. He hadn't minded catching a beautiful woman at the time. The force of her fall had pressed her body against his and what had happened to him was some sort of primal response that had taken control of his body before he'd realized it.

Mine, was the only coherent thought he'd managed to produce as he'd kept her on her feet. Hell, yeah, he'd responded. He was a man, after all.

But then he'd recognized her.

What was she on? And what would happen if she stumbled her way down the aisle?

This was a disaster of epic PR proportions. This woman was going to mess up all of his plans. And if he couldn't pull off this wedding, would he ever be able to truly call himself a Beaumont?

Phillip jerked him toward the table. "For the love of everything holy," he hissed in Matthew's ear, "be a gentleman."

Matthew shook him off. He had a few things he'd like to say to his brother and his future sister-in-law. "Why didn't you tell me?" he half whispered back at Phillip. "Do you know what this *means* for the wedding?"

On the other side of the room, Jo was at the fridge, getting the iced tea. Whitney stood next to her, head down and arms tucked around her slender waist.

For a second, he felt bad. Horrible, actually. The woman who stood thirty feet away from where he and Phillip were didn't look much like Whitney Wildz. Yes, she had Whitney's delicate bone structure and sweetheart face and yes, she had the jet-black hair with the telltale white streak in it. But her hair was cut into a neat pixie—no teased perm with blue and pink streaks. Her jeans and sweater fit her well and were quite tasteful—nothing like the ripped jeans and punk-rock T-shirts she'd always worn on the show. And she certainly wasn't acting strung out.

If it hadn't been for her face—and those pale green eyes, like polished jade, and that hair—he might not have recognized her.

But he did. Everything about him did.

"It means," Phillip whispered back, "that Jo's friend is here for the wedding. Whitney Maddox—she's a respected horse breeder. You will knock this crap off now or I'll—"

"You'll *what*? You haven't been able to beat me up since we were eight and you know it." Matthew tensed. He had a scant half inch on Phillip but he'd long ago learned to make the most of it.

Phillip grinned at him. It was not a kind thing on his face. "I'll turn Jo loose on you and trust me, buddy, that's a fate worse than death. Now knock it off and act like a decent human being."

There was something wrong about this. For so long, Matthew had been the one who scolded Phillip to straighten up and fly right. Phillip had been the one who didn't know how to act in polite company, who'd always found the most embarrassing thing to say and then said it. And it'd been Matthew who'd followed behind, cleaning up the messes, dealing with the headlines and soothing the ruffled feathers. That was what he did.

Briefly, Matthew wanted to be proud of his brother. He'd finally grown up.

But as wonderful as that was, it didn't change the fact that Whitney Wildz was not only going to be sitting down for dinner with them tonight, but she was also going to be in the Beaumont wedding.

He would have to rethink his entire strategy.

"Dinner," Jo called out. She sounded unnaturally perky about it. There was something odd about Jo being perky. It did nothing to help his mood.

"I really wish you had some beer in the house," he muttered to Phillip.

"Tough. Welcome to sobriety." Phillip led the way back to the table.

Matthew followed, trying to come up with a new game plan. He had a couple of options that he could see right off the bat. He could go with denial, just as Phillip and Jo seemed to be doing. This was Whitney Maddox. He had no knowledge of Whitney Wildz.

But that wasn't a good plan and he knew it. He'd recognized her, after all. Someone else was bound to do the same and the moment that someone did, it'd be all over. Yes, the list of celebrities who were attending this wedding was long but someone as scandalous as Whitney Wildz would create a stir no matter what she did.

He could go on the offensive. Send out a press release announcing that Whitney Wildz was the maid of honor. Hit the criticism head-on. If he did it early enough, he might defuse the situation—make it a nonissue by the big day. It could work.

Or it could blow up in his face. This wedding was about showing the world that the Beaumonts were above scandal— that they were stronger than ever. How was that going to happen now? Everything Whitney Wildz did was a scandal.

He took his seat. Whitney sat to his left, Phillip to his right. Jo's ridiculous little donkey sat on the floor in between him and Whitney. Good. Fine. At least he didn't have to look at Whitney, he reasoned. Just at Jo.

Who was not exactly thrilled with him. Phillip was right—Matthew was in no mood to have Jo turned loose on him. So he forced his best fake smile—the one he used when he was defusing some ticking time bomb created by one of his siblings. It always worked when he was talking to reporters.

He glanced at Phillip and then at Jo. Damn. The smile wasn't working on them.

He could *feel* Whitney sitting next to him. He didn't like that. He didn't want to be aware of her like that. He wasn't some teenager anymore, crushing in secret. He was a grown man with real problems.

Her.

But Phillip was staring daggers at him, and Jo looked as though she was going to stab him with the butter knife. So Matthew dug deep. He could be a gentleman. He could put on the Beaumont face no matter what. Being able to talk to a woman was part of the Beaumont legacy—a legacy he'd worked too hard to make his own. He wasn't about to let an unexpected blast from his past undermine everything he'd worked for. This wedding was about proving his legitimacy and that was that.

Phillip glared at him. Right. The wedding was about Phillip and Jo, too. And now their maid of honor.

God, what a mess.

"So, Whitney," Matthew began. She flinched when he said her name. He kept his voice pleasant and level. "What are you doing these days?"

Jo notched an eyebrow at him as she served the lasagna. *Hey*, he wanted to tell her. *I'm trying.*

Whitney smiled, but it didn't reach her eyes. "I raise horses." She took a piece of bread and passed the basket to him. She made sure not to touch him when she did it.

"Ah." That wasn't exactly a lot to go on, but it did explain how she and Jo knew each other, he guessed.

When Whitney didn't offer any other information, he asked, "What kind of horses?"

"Trakehners."

Matthew waited, but she didn't elaborate.

"One of her horses won gold in the World Equestrian Games," Phillip said. He followed up this observation with a swift kick to Matthew's shin.

Ow. Matthew grunted in pain but he managed not to curse out loud. "That's interesting."

"It's amazing," Phillip said. "Not even Dad could breed or buy a horse that took home gold." He leaned forward, turned on the Beaumont smile and aimed it squarely at Whitney.

Something flared in Matthew. He didn't like it when Phillip smiled at her like that.

"Trust me," Phillip continued, "he tried. Not winning

gold was one of his few failures as a horseman. That and not winning a Triple Crown."

Whitney cut Matthew a look out of the corner of her eye that hit him funny. Then she turned her attention to Phillip. "No one's perfect, right?"

"Not even Hardwick Beaumont," he agreed with a twinkle in his eye. "It turns out there are just some things money can't buy."

Whitney grinned. Suddenly, Matthew wanted to punch his brother—hard. This was normal enough—this was how Phillip talked to women. But seeing Whitney warm to him?

Phillip glanced at Matthew. *Be a gentleman*, he seemed to be saying. "Whitney's Trakehners are beautiful, highly trained animals. She's quite well-known in horse circles."

Whitney Wildz was well-known in horse circles? Matthew didn't remember any mention of that from the last article he'd read about her. Only that she'd made a spectacle of herself.

"How long have you been raising horses?"

"I bought my ranch eleven years ago." She focused her attention on her food. "After I left Hollywood."

So she really was Whitney Wildz. But...eleven years? That didn't seem right. It couldn't have been more than two years since the last headline.

"Where is your ranch?"

If Matthew had known who she really was, he would have done more digging. Be Prepared wasn't just a good Boy Scout motto—it was vital to succeeding in public relations.

One thing was abundantly clear. Matthew was not prepared for Whitney, whatever her last name was.

"Not too far from Bakersfield. It's very...quiet there."

Then she gazed up at him again. The look in her eyes stunned him—desperate for approval. He knew that look—he saw it in the mirror every morning.

Why would she want his approval? She was Whitney

Wildz, for crying out loud. She'd always done what she wanted, when she wanted—consequences be damned.

Except…nothing about her said she was out of control—except for the way she'd fallen into his arms.

His first instinct had been to hold her—to protect her. To claim her as his. What if…?

No.

There was no "what if" about this. His first duty was to his family—to making sure this wedding went off without a hitch. To making sure everyone knew that the Beaumonts were still in a position of power. To making sure he proved himself worthy of his father's legacy.

At the very least, he could be a gentleman about it.

"That's beautiful country," he said. Compliments were an important part of setting a woman at ease. If he were smart, he would have remembered that in the first place. "Your ranch must be lovely."

A touch of color brightened her cheeks. His stomach tensed. *She* was beautiful, he realized. Not the punk-rock hot she'd been back when he'd watched her show, but something delicate and ethereal.

Mine.

The word kept popping up in his head, completely unbidden. Which was ridiculous because the only thing Whitney was to him was a roadblock.

Phillip kicked him again. *Stop staring*, he mouthed at Matthew.

Matthew shook his head. He hadn't realized he was staring.

"Matthew, maybe we should discuss some of the wedding plans?" Jo said it nicely enough but there was no mistaking that question for an order.

"Of course," he agreed. The wedding. He needed to stay on track here. "We have an appointment with the seamstress tomorrow at ten. Jo, it's your final fitting. Whitney, we ordered your dress according to the measurements you sent in, but we've blocked out some additional time in case it requires additional fittings."

"That sounds fine," she said in a voice that almost sounded casual.

"Saturday night is the bachelorette party. I have a list of places that would be an appropriate location for you to choose from."

"I see," she said. She brushed her hand through her hair.

He fought the urge to do the same.

What was wrong with him? Seriously—*what* was wrong with him? He went from attracted to her to furious at everyone in the room and now he wanted to, what—stroke her hair? Claim her? Jesus, these were exactly the sort of impulses he'd always figured had ruled Phillip. The ones that had ruled their father. See a beautiful woman, act on the urge to sweep her off her feet. To hell with anything else.

Matthew needed to regain control of the situation—of himself—and fast.

"We'll need to get the shoes and jewelry squared away. We need to get you in to the stylist before then to decide how to deal with your hair, so we'll do that after the dress fitting." He waited, but she didn't say anything.

So he went on. "The rehearsal dinner is Tuesday night. Then the wedding is Christmas Eve, of course." A week and a half—that didn't leave him much time to deal with the disruption of Whitney Wildz. "The ladies will get manicures that morning before they get their hair done. Then we'll start with the photographs."

Whitney cleared her throat—but she still didn't meet his gaze. "Who else is in the wedding party?"

He wanted her to look at him—he wanted to get lost in her eyes. "Our older brother Chadwick will be walking with his wife, Serena. Frances and Byron will be walking together—they're twins, five years younger than I am." For a second,

Matthew had almost said *we*—as in he and Phillip. Because he and Phillip were only six months apart.

But he didn't want to bring his father's infidelity into this conversation, because that meant Whitney would know that he was the second choice, the child his father had never really loved. Or even acknowledged, for that matter. So he said *I.*

"That just leaves the two of us," he added, suddenly very interested in his plate. How was he going to keep this primal urge to haul her off under control if they were paired up for the wedding?

He could not let her distract him from his goals, no matter how much he wanted to. He had to pull this off—to prove that he was a legitimate Beaumont. Ravishing the maid of honor did not fall anywhere on his to-do list.

"Ah." He looked up when he heard her chair scrape against the floor. She stood and, without looking at him, said, "I'm a little tired from the drive. If you'll excuse me." Jo started to stand, but Whitney waved her off. "I think I can find my way."

Then she was gone, walking in a way that he could only describe as graceful. She didn't stumble and she didn't fall. She walked in a straight line for the stairs.

Several moments passed after she disappeared up the stairs. No one seemed willing to break the tense silence. Finally, Matthew couldn't take it anymore.

"What the *hell*? Why is Whitney Wildz your maid of honor and why didn't either of you see fit to tell me in advance? Jesus, if I'd known, I would have done things differently. Do you have any idea what the press will do when they find out?"

It was easier to focus on how this was going to screw up the wedding than on how his desire was on the verge of driving him mad.

"Gosh, I don't know. You think they'll make a big deal out of stuff that happened years ago and make Whitney feel like crap?" Phillip shot back. "You're right. That would really suck."

"Hey—this is not my fault. You guys sprung this on me."

"I believe," Jo said in a voice so icy it brought the temperature of the room down several degrees, "I told you I was asking Whitney Maddox to be my maid of honor. Whitney Wildz is a fictional character in a show that was canceled almost thirteen years ago. If you can't tell the difference between a real woman and a fictional teenager, then that's *your* problem, not hers."

"It *is* my problem," he got out through gritted teeth. "You can't tell me that's all in the past. What about the headlines?"

Phillip rolled his eyes. "Because everything the press prints is one hundred percent accurate, huh? I thought you, of all people, would know how the headlines can be manipulated."

"She's a normal person," Jo said. Instead of icy, though, she was almost pleading. "I retrained one of her horses and we got to spend time together last winter. She's a little bit of a klutz when she gets nervous but that's it. She's going to be fine."

"If *you* can treat her like a normal person," Phillip added. "Man—I thought you were this expert at reading people and telling them what they wanted to hear. What happened? Hit your head this morning or something?"

Matthew sat there, feeling stupid. Hell, he wasn't just feeling stupid—he *was* stupid. His first instinct had been to protect her. He should have stuck with it. He could do that without giving in to his desire to claim her, right?

Right. He was in control of his emotions. He could keep up a wall between the rest of the world and himself. He was good at it.

Then he made the mistake of glancing at that silly donkey, who gave him a baleful look of reproach. Great. Even the donkey was mad at him.

"I should apologize to her."

Phillip snorted. "You think?"

Damn it, he felt like a jerk. It didn't come naturally to him. Chadwick was the one who could be a royal pain simply because he wasn't clued in to the fact that most people had actual feelings. Phillip used to be an ass all the time because he was constantly drunk and horny. Matthew was the one who smoothed ruffled feathers and calmed everyone down.

Phillip was right. Matthew hadn't been reading the woman next to him. He'd been too busy thinking about old headlines and new lust to realize that she might want his approval.

"Which room is she in?"

Jo and Phillip shared a look before Phillip said, "Yours."

Three

Whitney found her room on the first try and shut the door behind her.

Well. So much for her little fantasy about a Christmas romance. She doubted that Matthew would have been less happy to see her if she'd thrown up on his shoes.

She flopped down on her bed and decided that she would not cry. Even though it was really tempting, she wouldn't. She'd learned long ago this was how it went, after all. People would treat her just fine until they recognized her and then? All bets were off. Once she'd been outed as Whitney Wildz, she might as well give up on normal. There was no going back.

She'd thought for a moment there she might get to do something ordinary—have a little Christmas romance between the maid of honor and the best man. But every time she got it in her foolish little head that she could be whoever she wanted to be…well, this was what would happen.

The thing was, she didn't even blame Matthew. Since he recognized her so quickly, that could only mean that he'd read some of the more recent headlines. Like the last time she'd tried to redeem Whitney Wildz by lending her notoriety to the Bakersfield Animal Shelter's annual fund-raising gala dinner. She'd been the keynote speaker—or would have been if she hadn't gotten the fancy Stuart Weitzman shoes she'd bought just for the occasion tangled up in the microphone cords on her way up to the podium.

The headlines had been unforgiving.

Whitney shivered. Boy, this was going to be a long, *cold* two weeks.

As she was getting up to turn her fireplace back on, she heard it—a firm knock.

Her brain diverted all energy from her legs to the question of who was on the other side of that door—Jo or a Beaumont?—and she tripped into the door with an audible *whump*.

Oh, for the love of everything holy. Just once—once!—she'd like to be able to walk and chew gum at the same time. She could sing and play the guitar simultaneously. She could do complicated dressage moves on the back of a one-ton animal. Why couldn't she put one foot in front of the other?

She forced herself to take a deep breath just as a male voice on the other side of the door said, "Is everything all right in there, Miss…uh…Ms. Maddox?"

Matthew. Great. How could this get worse? Let her count the ways. Had he come to ask her to drop out of the wedding? Or just threaten her to be on her best behavior?

She decided she would not cower. Jo had asked her to be in the wedding. If Jo asked her to drop out, she would. Otherwise, she was in. She collected her thoughts and opened the door a crack. "Yes, fine. Thanks."

Then she made the mistake of looking at him. God, it wasn't fair. It just *wasn't*.

Matthew Beaumont was, physically, the perfect man to have a Christmas romance with. He had to be about six foot one, broad chested, and that chin? Those eyes? Even his deep red hair made him look distinctive. Striking.

Gorgeous.

Too darned bad he was an ass.

"Can I help you?" she asked, determined to be polite if it killed her. She would not throw a diva fit and prove him right. Even if there would be a certain amount of satisfaction in slamming the door in his face.

He gave her a grin that walked the fine line between awkward and cute. He might be even better-looking than his brother, but he appeared to possess none of the charm. "Look, Ms. Maddox—"

"Whitney."

"Oh. Okay. Whitney. We got off on the wrong foot and—"

She winced.

He paused. "*I* got off on the wrong foot. And I want to apologize to you." His voice was strong, exuding confidence. It made everything about him that much sexier.

She blinked at him. "What?"

"I jumped to conclusions when I realized who you were and I apologize for that." He waited for her to say something but she had nothing.

Was he serious? He looked serious. He wasn't biting back laughter or— She glanced down at his hands. They were tucked into the pockets of his gray wool trousers. No, he wasn't about to snap an awful photo of her to post online, either.

He pulled his hands from his pockets and held them at waist level, open palms up, as if he knew what she was thinking. "It's just that this wedding is incredibly important for rebuilding the public image of the Beaumont family and it's my job to make sure everyone stays on message."

"The…public image?" She leaned against the door, staring up at him. Maybe he wasn't a real man—far too handsome to be one. And he was certainly talking like a space alien. "I thought this was about Jo and Phillip getting married."

"That, too," he hurried to agree. This time, his smile was a little more charming, like something a politician might pull out when he needed to win an argument. "I just— Look. I just want to make sure that we don't make headlines for the wrong reason."

Embarrassment flamed down the back of her neck. She looked away. He was trying to be nice by saying *we* but they both knew that he meant *her*.

"I know you don't believe this, but I have absolutely no desire to make headlines. At all. Ever. If no one else recognized me for the rest of my life, that'd be super."

There was a moment of silence that was in danger of becoming painful. "Whitney…"

The way he said her name—soft and tender and almost reverent—dragged her eyes up to his. The look in his eyes hit her like a bolt out of, well, the blue. He had the most amazing eyes…

For that sparkling moment, it almost felt as if…as if he was going to say something that could be construed as romantic. Something that didn't make her feel as though the weight of this entire event were being carried on her shoulders.

She wanted to hear something that made her feel like Whitney Maddox—that being Whitney Maddox was a good thing. A great thing. And she wanted to hear that something come out of Matthew's mouth, in that voice that could melt away the chilly winter air. Desire seemed to fill the space between them.

She leaned toward him. She couldn't help it. At the same time, his mouth opened as one of his hands moved. Then, just as soon as the motion had started, it stopped. His mouth closed and he appeared to shake himself. "I'll meet you at the dress fitting tomorrow. To make sure everything's—"

"On message?"

He notched up an eyebrow. She couldn't tell if she'd offended him or amused him. Or both. "Perfect," he corrected. "I just want it to be perfect."

"Right." There would be no sweet words. If there was one thing she wasn't, it was perfect. "Will it just be you?"

He gave her a look that was surprisingly wounded. She couldn't help but grin at him, which earned her a smile that looked more…real, somehow. As though what had just passed between them was almost…flirting.

"No. The wedding planner will be joining us—and the seamstress and her assistants, of course."

"Of course." She leaned against the door. Were they flirting? Or was he charming her because that was what all Beaumonts did?

God, he was *so* handsome. He exuded raw power. She had no doubt that whatever he said went.

A man like him would be hard to resist.

"Tomorrow, then," she said.

"I look forward to it." He gave her a tight smile before he turned away. Just as she was shutting the door, he turned back. "Whitney," he said again in that same deep, confident and—she hoped—sincere voice. "It truly is a pleasure to meet you."

Then he was gone.

She shut the door.

Heavens. It was going to be a *very* interesting two weeks.

"So," Whitney began as they passed streetlights decorated like candy canes. The drive had, thus far, been quiet. "Who's on the guest list again?"

"The Beaumonts," Jo said with a sigh. "Hardwick Beaumont's four ex-wives—"

"Four?"

Jo nodded as she tapped on the steering wheel. "All nine of Phillip's siblings and half siblings will be there, although only the four he actually grew up with are in the wedding—Chadwick, Matthew, Frances and Byron."

Whitney whistled. "That's a *lot* of kids." Part of why she'd loved doing the show was that, for the first time, she'd felt as though she'd had a family, one with brothers and sisters and parents who cared about her. Even if it were all just pretend, it was still better than being the only child Jade Maddox focused on with a laserlike intensity.

But ten kids? *Dang.*

"And that doesn't count the illegitimate ones," Jo said in a conspiratorial tone. "Phillip says they know of three, but there could be more. The youngest is…nineteen, I think."

As much as she hated gossip… "Seriously? Did that man not know about condoms?"

"Didn't care," Jo said. "Between you and me, Hardwick Beaumont was an old-fashioned misogynist. Women were solely there for his entertainment. Anything else that happened was their problem, not his."

"Sounds like a real jerk."

"I understand he was a hell of a businessman, but…yeah. On the whole, his kids aren't that bad. Chadwick's a tough nut to crack, but his wife, Serena, balances him out really well. Phillip's… Well, Phillip's Phillip." She grinned one of those private grins that made Whitney blush. "Matthew can come on a bit strong but really, he's a good guy. He's just wound a bit tight. Very concerned with the family's image. It's like…he wants everything to be perfect."

"I noticed." Whitney knew she was talking about the coming-on-strong part, but her brain immediately veered back to when she'd stumbled into his arms. His strong arms.

And then there was the conversation they'd had—the private one. The one that could have been flirting. And the way he'd said her name…

"We're really sorry about last night," Jo repeated for about the fifteenth time.

"No worries," Whitney hurried to say. "He apologized."

"Matthew is…very good at what he does. He just needs to lighten up a little bit. Have some fun."

She wondered at that. Would fun be a part of this? The dinner had said no. But the conversation after? She had no idea. If only she weren't so woefully out of practice at flirting.

"I can still drop out," she said. "If that'll make it simpler."

Jo laughed—not an awkward sound, but one that was

truly humorous. "You're kidding, right? Did I mention the ex-wives? You know who else is going to be here?"

"No…"

"The crown prince of Belgravitas."

"You're kidding, right?" God, she hoped Jo was kidding. She didn't want to make a fool of herself in front of honest-to-God royalty.

"Nope. His wife, the princess Susanna, used to date Phillip."

"Get *out*."

"I'm serious. Drake—the rapper—will be there, as well. He and Phillip are friends. Jay Z and Beyoncé had a scheduling conflict, but—"

"Seriously?" It wasn't as though she didn't know that Phillip Beaumont was a famous guy—all those commercials, all those stories about parties he hosted at music festivals—but this was crazy.

"If you drop out," Jo went on, "who on earth am I going to get to replace you? Out of the two hundred people who'll be at the wedding and the six hundred who'll be at the reception, you know how many I invited? My parents, my grandma Lina, my uncle Larry and aunt Penny, and my parents' neighbors. Eleven people. That's it. That's all I have. And you."

Whitney didn't know what to say. She didn't want to do this, not after last night. But Jo was one of her few friends. Someone who didn't care about Whitney Wildz or *Growing Up Wildz* or even that horrible Christmas album she'd put out, *Whitney Wildz Sings Christmas, Yo.*

She didn't want to disappoint her friend.

"Honestly," Jo said, "there's going to be so many egos on display that I doubt people will even realize who you are. Don't take that the wrong way."

"I won't," Whitney said with a smile. She could do this. She could pull off normal for a few weeks. She couldn't compete with that guest list. She was just the maid of honor. Who would notice her, anyway? Besides Matthew, that was…

"And you're right. It won't be like that last fund-raiser."

"Exactly," Jo said, sounding encouraging. "You were the headliner there—of course people were watching you. Matthew only acted like he did because he's a perfectionist. I truly believe you'll be fine." She pulled into a parking lot. "It'll be fine."

"All right," Whitney agreed. She didn't quite believe the sentiment but she couldn't disappoint Jo. "It will be fine."

"Good."

They got out. Whitney stared at the facade of the Bridal Collection. This was it. Once she was in the dress, there was no backing out.

Oh, who was she kidding? There was no backing out anyway. Jo was right. They were the kind of people who didn't have huge social circles or celebrities on speed dial. They were horse people. She and Jo got along only because they both loved animals and they both had changed their ways.

"You're really having a wedding with Grammy winners and crown princes?"

"Yup," Jo said, shaking her head. "Honestly, though, it's not the over-the-top wedding that matters. It's the marriage. Besides," she added as they went inside, "David Guetta is going to be doing the music for the reception. How cool is that?"

"Pretty cool," Whitney agreed. She didn't recognize the name, but then, why would she? She wasn't famous anymore.

Maybe Jo was right. No one would care about her. She'd managed to stay out of the headlines for almost three years, after all—that was a lifetime in today's 24/7 news cycle. In that time, there'd been other former teen stars who'd grabbed much bigger headlines for much more scandalous reasons.

They walked into the boutique to find Matthew pacing between rows of frothy white dresses and decorations that were probably supposed to be Christmas trees but really looked more as though someone had dipped pipe cleaners in glitter. The whole place was so bright it made her eyes hurt.

Matthew—wearing dark gray trousers and a button-up shirt with a red tie under his deep green sweater—was so out of place that she couldn't *not* look at him. She wouldn't have thought it possible, but he looked even better today than he had the other night. As she appreciated all the goodness that was Matthew Beaumont, he looked up from his phone.

Their eyes met, and her breath caught in her throat. The warmth in his eyes, the curve to his lips, the arch in his eyebrow—heat flooded Whitney's cheeks. Was he happy to see her? Or was she misreading the signals?

Then he glanced at Jo. "Ladies," he said in that confident tone of his. It should have seemed wholly out of place in the midst of this many wedding gowns, but on him? "I was just about to call. Jo, they're waiting for you."

"Where's the wedding planner?" Whitney asked. If the planner wasn't here, then she and Jo weren't late. Late was being the last one in.

"Getting Jo's dress ready."

Dang. Whitney tried to give her friend a smile that was more confident than she actually felt. Jo threaded her way back through racks of dresses and disappeared into a room.

Then Whitney and Matthew were alone. Were they still almost flirting? Or were they back to where they'd been at dinner? If only she hadn't fallen into him. If only he hadn't recognized her. If only…

"Is there someone else who can help me try my dress on?"

"Jo's dress requires several people to get her into it," he said. Then he bowed and pointed the way. "Your things are in here."

"Thanks." She held her head high as she walked past him.

"You're welcome." His voice trickled over her skin like a cool stream of water on a too-hot day.

She stepped into a dressing room—thankfully, one with a door. Once she had that door shut, she sagged against it. That voice, that face were even better today than they'd been last night. Last night, he'd been trying to cover his surprise and anger. Today? Today he just looked happy to see her.

She looked at the room she'd essentially locked herself in. It was big enough for a small love seat and a padded ottoman. A raised dais stood in front of a three-way mirror.

And there, next to the mirrors, hung a dress. It was a beautiful dove-gray silk gown—floor length, of course. Sleeveless, with sheer gathered silk forming one strap on the left side. The hemline was flared so that it would flow when she walked down the aisle, no doubt.

It was stunning. Even back when she'd walked the red carpet, she'd never worn a dress as sophisticated as this. When she was still working on *Growing Up Wildz*, she'd had to dress modestly—no strapless, no deep necklines. And when she'd broken free of all the restrictions that had hemmed her in for years, well, "classic" hadn't been on her to-do list. She'd gone for shock value. Short skirts. Shorter skirts. Black. Torn shirts that flashed her chest. Offensive slogans. Safety pins holding things together. Anything she could come up with to show that she wasn't a squeaky-clean kid anymore.

And it'd worked. Maybe too well.

She ran her hands over the silk. It was cool, smooth. If a dress could feel beautiful, this did. A flicker of excitement started to build. Once, before it'd been a chore, she'd liked to play dress-up. Maybe this would be fun. She hoped.

Several pairs of shoes dyed to match were lined up next to the dress—some with four-inch heels. Whitney swallowed hard. There'd be no way she could walk down the aisle in those beauties and not fall flat on her face.

Might as well get this over with. She stripped off her parka and sweater, then the boots and jeans. She caught a glimpse of herself in the three-way mirror—hard not to with those angles. Ugh. The socks had to go. And…

Her bra had straps. The dress did not.

She shucked the socks and, before she could think better about it, the bra. Then she hurried into the dress, trying not to pull on the zipper as the silk slipped over her head with a shushing sound.

The fabric puddled at her feet as she tried to get the zipper pulled up, but her arms wouldn't bend in that direction. "I need help," she called out, praying that an employee or a seamstress or anyone besides Matthew Beaumont was out there.

"Is it safe to come in?" Matthew asked from the other side of the door.

Oh, no. Whitney made another grab at the zipper, but nothing happened except her elbow popped. *Ow.* She checked her appearance. Her breasts were covered. It was just the zipper.…

"Yes."

The door opened and Matthew walked in. To his credit, he didn't enter as if he owned the place. He came in with his eyes cast down before he took a cautious glance around. When he spotted her mostly covered, the strangest smile tried to crack his face. "Ah, there you are."

"Here I am," she agreed, wondering where else on earth he thought she could have gotten off to in the ten minutes she'd been in here. "I can't get the zipper up all the way."

She really didn't know what to expect at this point. The majority of her interactions with Matthew ranged from outright rude to surly. But then, just when she was about to write him off as a jerk and nothing more, he'd do something that set her head spinning again.

Like right now. He walked up to her and held out his hand, as if he were asking her to dance.

Even in the cramped dressing room, he was impossibly

handsome. But he'd already muddled her thoughts—mean one moment, sincere the next. She didn't want to let anything physical between them confuse her even further.

When she didn't put her hand in his, he said, "Just to step up on the dais," as if he could read her thoughts.

She took his hand. It was warm and strong, just as his arms had been. He guided her up the small step and then to the middle. "Ah, shoes," he said. Then he let her go.

"No—just the zipper," she told him, but he was already back by the shoes, looking at them.

Lord. She knew what was about to happen. She was all of five-four on a good day. He would pick the four-inch heels in an attempt to get her closer to Jo's height. And then she'd either have to swallow her pride and tell him she couldn't walk in them or risk tripping down the aisle on the big day.

"These should work," he said, picking up the pair of peep-toed shoes with the stacked heel only two inches high. "Try these on."

"If you could just zip me up first. *Please.*" The last thing she wanted to do was wobble in those shoes and lose the grip she had on the front of her dress.

He carried the shoes over to her and set them on the ground. Then he stood.

This time, when his gaze traveled over her, it didn't feel as if he were dismissing her, as he had the first time. Far from it. Instead, this time it was almost as if he was appreciating what he saw.

Maybe.

She felt him grab the edges of the dress and pull them together. Something about this felt…intimate. Almost too intimate. It blew way past possible flirting. She closed her eyes. Then, slowly, the zipper clicked up tooth by tooth.

Heat radiated down her back, warming her from the inside out. She breathed in, then out, feeling the silk move over her bare flesh. Matthew was so close she could smell his cologne—something light, with notes of sandalwood. Heat built low in her back—warm, luxurious heat that made her want to slowly turn in his arms and stop caring whether or not the dress zipped at all.

She could do it. She could hit on the best man and find out what had been behind that little conversation they'd had in private last night. And this time, she wouldn't trip.

Except…except for his first reaction to her—if she hit on him, he might assume she was out to ruin his perfect wedding or something. So she did nothing. Matthew zipped the dress all the way up. Then she felt his hands smoothing down the pleats in the back, then adjusting the sheer shoulder strap.

She stopped breathing as his hands skimmed over her.

This had to be nothing. This was only a control freak obsessively making sure every detail, every single pleat, was perfect. His touch had nothing to do with *her*.

She felt him step around her until he was standing by her side. "Aren't you going to look?" he asked, his voice warm and, if she didn't know any better, inviting.

She could feel him waiting right next to her, the heat from his body contrasting with the cool temperature of the room. So she opened her eyes. What else could she do?

The sight that greeted her caused her to gasp. An elegant, sophisticated woman stood next to a handsome, powerful man. She knew that was her reflection in the mirror, but it didn't look like her.

"Almost perfect," Matthew all but sighed in satisfaction. *Almost.* What a horrible word.

"It's amazing." She fought the urge to twirl. Someone as buttoned-up as Matthew probably wouldn't appreciate a good twirl.

The man in the reflection grinned at her—a real grin, one that crinkled the edges of his eyes. "It's too long on you. Let's try the shoes." Then, to her amazement, he knelt down and held out a shoe for her, as if this were some backward version of *Cinderella*.

Whitney lifted up her skirt and gingerly stepped into the shoe. It felt solid and stable—not like the last pair of fancy shoes she'd tried to walk in.

She stepped into the other shoe, trying not to think about how Matthew was essentially face-to-knee or how she was in significant danger of snagging these pretty shoes on the edge of the dais and going down in a blaze of glory.

When she had both shoes firmly on, Matthew sat back. "How do those feel?"

"Not bad," she admitted. She took a preliminary step back. "Pretty good, actually."

"Can you walk in them? Or do you need a ballerina flat?"

She gaped at him. Of all the things he might have asked her, that wasn't even on the list. Then it hit her. "Jo told you I was a klutz, right?"

He grinned again. It did some amazing things to his face, which, in turn, did some amazing things to the way a lazy sort of heat coiled around the base of her spine and began to pulse.

"She might have mentioned it."

Whitney shouldn't have been embarrassed, and if she was, it shouldn't have bothered her anymore. Embarrassment was second nature for her now, as ordinary as breathing oxygen.

But it did. "Because you thought I was drunk."

His Adam's apple bobbed, but he didn't come back with the silky smile he'd pulled out on her last night, the one that made her feel as if she was being managed.

"In the interest of transparency, I also considered the option that you might have been stoned."

Four

Whitney blinked down at him, her delicate features pulled tight. Then, without another word, she turned back to the mirror.

What happened? Matthew stood, letting his gaze travel over her. She was, for lack of a better word, stunning. "The color suits you," he said, hoping a compliment would help.

It didn't. She rolled her eyes.

Transparency had always worked before. He'd thought that his little admission would come out as an ironic joke, something they could both chuckle over while he covertly admired the figure she cut in that dress.

What was it about this woman that had him sticking his foot in his mouth at every available turn?

It was just because she wasn't what he'd been expecting, that was all. He'd been up late last night, digging into the not-sordid-at-all history of Whitney Maddox, trying to get his feet out of his mouth and back under his legs. She *was* a respected horse breeder. Her horses *were* beautiful animals and that one *had* won a gold medal. But there weren't any pictures of Whitney Maddox anywhere—not on her ranch's website, not on any social media. Whitney Maddox was like a ghost—there but not there.

Except the woman before him was very much here. His hands still tingled from zipping her into that dress, from the glimpse of her panties right where the zipper had ended. How he itched to unzip it, to expose the bare skin he'd seen but not touched—slip those panties off her hips.

He needed to focus on what was important here, and that was making sure that this woman—no matter what name she went by—did not pull this wedding off message. That she did not pull *him* off message. That was what he had to think about. Not the way the dress skimmed over her curves or the way her dark hair made her stand out.

Before he knew what he was doing, he said, "You look beautiful in that dress."

This time, she didn't roll her eyes. She gave him the kind of look that made it clear she didn't believe him.

"You can see that, right? You're stunning."

She stared at him for a moment longer. "You're confusing me," she said.

She had a sweet smell to her, something with warm vanilla notes overlaying a deeper spice. Good enough to eat, he thought, suddenly fascinated with the curve of her neck. He could press his lips against her skin and watch her reaction in the mirror. Would she blush? Pull away? Or lean into his touch?

She looked away. "I could change my hair."

"What?"

"I could try to dye it all blond, although," she said with a rueful smile, "it didn't turn out so well the last time I tried it. The white streak won't take dye, for some reason. God knows I've tried to color it over, but it doesn't work. It's blond or nothing."

"Why on God's green earth would you want to dye your hair?"

He couldn't see her as a blonde. It would be wrong on so many levels. It'd take everything that was fine and delicate about her and make it washed-out, like a painting left out in the rain.

"If I'm blonde, no one will recognize me. No one would ever guess that Whitney Wildz is standing up there. That way, if I trip in the shoes or drop my bouquet, people will just think I'm a klutz and not assume I'm stoned. Like they always do."

Shame sucker punched him in the gut. "Don't change your hair." He reached out and brushed the edge of her bangs away from her face.

She didn't lean away from him, but she didn't lean into him, either. He didn't know if that was a good thing or not.

"But…" She swallowed and tried to look tough. She didn't make it. "I look like me. People will *recognize* me. I thought you didn't want that to happen."

"You say that as if looking like yourself is a bad thing."

In the mirror's reflection, her gaze cut to him. "Isn't it?"

He took a step closer to her, close enough that he could slide his fingers from the fringe of her hair down her neck, down her arm. He couldn't help it, which was something outside of his experience entirely. He'd *always* been able to help himself. He'd never allowed himself to get swept up in something as temporary, as fleeting, as emotional attraction. He'd witnessed firsthand what acting on attraction could do, how it could ruin marriages, leave bastard babies behind— leave children forgotten.

With the specter of his father hovering around him, Matthew managed to find some of the restraint that normally came so easy to him. He didn't slide his hand down her bare arm or pull her into his chest. Instead, he held himself to arranging the shoulder of the dress. She watched him in the mirror, her eyes wide. "You are *beautiful*," he said. It came out like something Phillip would say—low and seductive. It didn't sound like Matthew talking at all.

She sucked in a deep breath, which, from his angle, did

enticing things to her chest. He wanted to sweep her into his arms. He wanted to tell her he'd had a crush on her back in the day. He wanted to get her out of that dress and into his bed.

He did none of those things.

Focus, damn it.

He took a step back and tried his hardest to look at her objectively. The heels helped, but the hem of the dress still puddled around her. She'd need it hemmed, but they had to settle on the shoes first.

"Let's see how you walk in those." There. That was something that wasn't a come-on and wasn't a condemnation. Footwear was a safe choice at this point.

She stood for a moment, as if she was trying to decide what his motivations were. So he held out his arm for her. He could do that. She'd walk back down the aisle on his arm after the ceremony. Best they get used to it now.

After a brief pause, she slipped her hand around his elbow and, after gathering her skirts in one hand, stepped off the dais. They moved toward the door, where he opened it for her.

She walked ahead of him, the dress billowing around her legs just as he'd wanted it to. The salon had a bouquet of artificial flowers on a nearby table. He handed them to her. "Slow steps, big smile."

"Right," she said, an odd grin pulling up at the corners of her mouth. "No skipping. Got it."

She walked down the aisle, then turned and came back toward him with a big fake smile on her face. Then, just as she almost reached him, the toe of her shoe caught in the too-long hem of the dress and she stumbled. The bouquet went flying.

He caught her. He had to, right? It wasn't about pulling her into his arms. This was a matter of personal safety.

He had her by her upper arms. "Sorry," she muttered as he pulled her back onto her feet.

"Don't worry about it."

She gave him a hard look, her body rigid under his hands. "I had to worry about it yesterday. You're sure I'm not on anything today?"

Okay, yes, he deserved that. That didn't make it any less sucky to have it thrown back in his face.

Without letting go of her, he leaned down and inhaled deeply. "No trace of alcohol on your breath," he said, staring at her lips.

She gasped.

Then he removed one of his hands from her arm and used it to tilt her head back until she had no choice but to look him in the eyes.

Years of dealing with Phillip while he was drunk had taught Matthew what the signs were. "You're not on anything."

"You…can tell?"

He should let her go. She had her balance back. She didn't need him to hold her up and she certainly didn't need him to keep a hand under her chin.

But he didn't. Instead, he let his fingers glide over her smooth skin. "When you become a Beaumont, you develop certain skills to help you survive."

She blinked at him. "When you *become* a Beaumont? What does that mean? Aren't you a Beaumont?"

Matthew froze. Had he really said that? Out loud? He *never* drew attention to his place in the family, *never* said anything that would cast doubt on his legitimacy. Hell, his whole life had been about proving to the whole world that he was a Beaumont through and through.

What was it about this woman that made him stick his foot into his mouth?

Whitney stared at him. "You're confusing me again,"

she repeated, her voice a whisper that managed to move his heart rate up several notches. Her lips parted as she ever so slightly leaned into his hand.

"You're the one who's confusing me," he whispered back as he stroked his fingertips against her skin. For a woman who was neither here nor there, she was warm and solid and so, *so* soft under his hands.

"Then I guess we're even?" She looked up at him with those pale green eyes. He was going to kiss her. Long. Hard. He was going to taste her sweetness, feel her body as it pressed against his and—

"Whitney? Matthew?"

Jo's voice cut through the insanity he'd been on the brink of committing. He let go of Whitney, only to grab her immediately when she took a step back and stepped on her hem again.

"I've got you," he told her.

"Repeatedly," she said. He couldn't tell if she was amused or not.

Then Jo came around the corner, seamstresses and salon employees trailing her. She pulled up short when she saw the two of them and said, "I need to go," as the wedding planner started unfastening the back of her dress.

"What?" Matthew said.

"Why?" Whitney said at the same time.

"A mare I'm training out on the farm is having a meltdown and Richard is afraid she's going to hurt herself." She looked over her shoulder at the small army of women who were attempting to get her out of her dress. "Can you go any faster?"

There were murmurs of protest from the seamstresses as the wedding planner said, "We can't risk tearing the dress, Ms. Spears."

Jo sighed heavily.

Whitney and Matthew took advantage of the distraction

to separate. "I'll come with you," Whitney said. "I can help. You taught me what to do."

"No, you won't," he said.

It must have come out a little harsher than he meant it to, because every woman in the room—all six of them—stopped and looked at him. "I mean," he added, softening his tone, "we have too much to do. We have to get your dress hemmed, we have an appointment with the stylist this afternoon— everyone is set except you. We *must* keep your schedule."

There was a moment of silence, broken only by the sound of Jo's dress rustling as the seamstresses worked to free her from the elaborate confines.

Whitney wasn't looking at him. She was looking at Jo. She'd do whatever Jo said, he realized. Not what he said. He wasn't used to having his orders questioned. Everyone else in the family had long ago realized that Matthew was always right.

"Matthew is right," Jo said. "Besides, having a new person show up will only freak out Rapunzel. I need to do this alone."

"Oh," Whitney said as if Jo had just condemned her to swing from the gallows. "All right."

"Your dress is amazing," Jo said, clearly trying to smooth over the ruffled feathers.

"Yours, too," Whitney replied. Jo's compliment must have helped, because Whitney already sounded better.

That was another thing Matthew wasn't expecting from Whitney Wildz. A willingness to work? A complete lack of interest in throwing a diva fit when things didn't go her way?

She confused him, all right. He'd never met a woman who turned his head around as fast and as often as Whitney did. Not even the celebrities and socialites he'd known made him dizzy the way she did. Sure, such women made plays for him—he was a Beaumont and a good-looking man. But none of them distracted him from his goal. None of them got him off message.

He tried telling himself it was just because he'd liked her so many years ago. This was merely the lingering effects of a crush run amok. His teenage self was screwing with his adult self. That was all. It didn't matter that Whitney today was a vision in that dress—far more beautiful than anything he'd ever imagined back in the day. He had a job to do—a wedding to pull off, a family image to rescue, his rightful place to secure. His adult self was in charge here.

No matter what the Beaumonts put their minds to, they would always come out on top. That'd been the way Hardwick Beaumont had run his business and his family. He'd amassed a huge personal fortune and a legacy that had permanently reshaped Denver—and, one could argue, America. He expected perfection and got it—or else.

Even though Chadwick had sold the Beaumont Brewery, even though Phillip had crashed and burned in public, Matthew was still standing tall. He'd weathered those storms and he would pull this wedding off.

"There," one of the seamstresses said. "Mind the edge…"

Jo clutched at the front of the dress. "Matthew, if you don't mind."

Right. He turned his back to her so she could step out of the $15,000 dress they'd chosen because it made Jo, the tomboy cowgirl, look like a movie-star goddess, complete with the fishtail bodice and ten-foot-long train. The Beaumonts were about glamour and power. Every single detail of this wedding had to reflect that. Then no one would ever question his place in the family again.

Not even the maid of honor.

He looked down at Whitney out of the corner of his eye. She was right. With her fine bone structure, jet-black hair with the white stripe and those large eyes, he could dress her in a burlap sack and she'd still be instantly recognizable. The dress only made her features stand out that much more.

So why hadn't he agreed that a drastic change to her hair was a good idea?

It'd be like painting pouty ruby-red lips on the *Mona Lisa.* It'd just be wrong.

Still, he felt as if he'd done very little but insult her in the past twenty-four hours, and no matter what his personal feelings about Whitney were, constantly berating a member of the wedding party was not the way to ensure things stayed on message.

"I'll take you to lunch," he offered. "We'll make a day of it."

She gave him the side eye. "You normally spend your day styling women for weddings?"

"No," he said with a grin. "Far from it. I'm just making sure everything is—"

"Perfect."

"Exactly."

She tilted her head to one side and touched her cheek with a single fingertip. "Aren't you going to miss work?"

"This is my job." Again, he got the side eye, so he added, "I do the PR for Percheron Drafts, the beer company Chadwick started after he sold the Beaumont Brewery." He'd convinced Chadwick that the wedding needed to be a showcase event first. It hadn't been that hard. His older brother had learned to trust his instincts in the business world, and Matthew's instincts told him that marrying former playboy bachelor Phillip Beaumont off in a high-profile high-society wedding would pay for itself in good publicity.

Convincing Phillip and Jo that their wedding was going to be over-the-top in every possible regard, however, had been another matter entirely.

"I see," she said in a way that made it pretty clear she

didn't. Then she cleared her throat. "Won't your girlfriend be upset if you take me out to lunch?"

That was what she said. What she meant, though, was something entirely different. To his ears, it sure sounded as though she'd asked if he had really been about to kiss her earlier and whether he might try it again.

He leaned toward her, close enough he caught the scent of vanilla again. "I'm not involved with anyone," he said. What he meant?

Yeah, he might try kissing her again. Preferably someplace where seamstresses wouldn't bust in on them.

He watched the blush warm her skin. Again, his fingers itched to unzip that dress—to touch her. But... "You?"

His web searches last night hadn't turned up anything that suggested she was in a relationship.

She looked down at the floor. "I find it's best if I keep to myself. Less trouble that way."

"Then lunch won't be a problem."

"Are you sure? Or will you need to search my bag for illegal contraband?"

Ouch. Her dig stung all the more because he'd earned it. Really, there was only one way to save face here—throw himself on his sword. If he were lucky, she'd have mercy on him. "I'm sure. I'm done being an ass about things."

She jolted, her mouth curving into a smile that, no matter how hard she tried, she couldn't repress. "Can I have that in writing?"

"I could even get it notarized, if that's what it'd take for you to forgive me."

She looked at him then, her eyes full of wonder. "You already apologized last night. You don't have to do it again."

"Yes, I do. I keep confusing you. It's ungentlemanly."

Her eyebrows jumped up as her mouth opened but behind them, someone cleared her throat. "Mr. Beaumont? We're ready to start on Ms. Maddox's dress."

Whitney's mouth snapped shut as that blush crept over her cheeks. Matthew looked around. Jo and her dress were nowhere to be seen. He and Whitney had been standing by themselves in the middle of the salon for God knows how long, chatting. Flirting.

Right. They had work to do here.

But he was looking forward to lunch.

Five

"I'm sorry, sir, but the only seats we have are the window seats," the hostess said.

Matthew turned to look at Whitney. He hadn't expected Table 6 to be this crowded. He'd thought he was taking her to a quiet restaurant where they could talk. Where he could look at her over a table with only the bare minimum interruption.

But the place was hopping with Christmas shoppers taking a break. Shopping bags crowded the aisle, and there were more than a few people wearing elf hats and reindeer antlers. The hum of conversation was so loud he almost couldn't hear Bing Crosby crooning Christmas carols on the sound system.

"We can go someplace else," he offered to Whitney.

She pulled down her sunglasses and shot him a look, as if he'd dared her to throw a diva fit. "This is fine."

Matthew glanced around the restaurant again. He really didn't want to sit at a bar-high counter next to her. On the other hand, then he could maybe brush against her arm, her thigh.

They took the only two spots left in the whole place. A shaft of sunlight warmed their faces. Whitney took off her sunglasses and her knit hat and turned her face to the light.

She exhaled, a look of serene joy radiating from her. She was so beautiful, so unassuming, that she simply took his breath away.

Then it stopped. She shook back to herself and gave him an embarrassed look. "Sorry," she said, patting her hair back into place. "It's a lot colder here than it is in California. I miss the sun."

"Don't apologize." Her cheeks colored under his gaze. "Let's order. Then tell me about California." She notched a delicate eyebrow at him in challenge. "And I mean more than the basics. I want to know about *you*."

The corners of her mouth curved up as she nodded. But the waitress came, so they turned their attention to the daily specials. She ordered the soup and salad. He picked the steak sandwich. The process seemed relatively painless.

But Matthew noticed the way the waitress's eyes had widened as Whitney had asked about the soup du jour. *Oh, no*, he thought. The woman had recognized her.

Maybe it wouldn't be a problem. The restaurant was busy, after all. The staff had better things to do than wonder why Whitney Wildz had suddenly appeared at the counter, right?

He turned his attention back to Whitney. Which was not easy to do, crammed into the two seats in this window. But he managed to pull it off. "Now," he said, fixing her with what he really hoped wasn't a wolfish gaze, "tell me about you."

She shrugged.

The waitress came back with some waters and their coffee. "Anything else?" she asked with an ultraperky smile.

"No," Matthew said forcefully. "Thank you."

The woman's eyes cut back to Whitney again and she grinned in disbelief as she walked away. Oh, hell.

But Whitney hadn't noticed. She'd unwrapped her straw and was now wrapping the paper around her fingers, over and over.

Matthew got caught up in watching her long fingers bend the wrapper again and again and forgot about the waitress.

"You're confusing me," she said, staring hard at her scrap of paper. "Again."

"How?" She gave him the side eye. "No, seriously—please tell me. It's not my job here to confuse you."

She seemed to deflate, just a little. But it didn't last. "You're looking at me like that."

He forced his attention to his own straw. Hopefully, that would give her the space she needed. "Like how?"

The silence stretched between them like a string pulling tight. He was afraid he might snap. And he never snapped. He was unsnappable, for God's sake.

But then his mind flashed back to the bare skin of her back, how the zipper had ended just at the waistband of her panties. All he'd seen was a pretty edge of lace. Now he couldn't get his mind off it.

"I can't decide if you think I'm the biggest pain in the neck of your life or if you're— If you—" She exhaled, the words coming out in a rush. "If you like me. And when you look at me like that, it just…makes it worse."

"I can't help it," he admitted. It was easier to say that without looking at her. Maybe this counter seating wasn't all bad.

Her hands stilled. "Why not?" There was something else in her voice. That something seemed to match the look she'd given him last night, the one that craved his approval.

He couldn't tell her why not. Not without telling her… what? That he'd nursed a boyhood crush on her long after he'd left boyhood behind? That he'd followed her in the news? That this very afternoon, she'd been the most beautiful woman he'd ever seen?

"Tell me about you," he said, praying that she'd go along with the subject change. "Tell me about your life."

He felt her gaze on him. Now it was his turn to blush. "If I do, will you tell me about you?"

He nodded.

"Okay," she agreed. He expected her to begin twisting her paper again, but she didn't. She dug out her phone. "This is Pride and Joy," she said, showing him a horse and rider holding a gold medal.

The picture was her phone's wallpaper. Her pride and joy, indeed. "That was the Games, right?"

"Right." Her tone brightened considerably at his memory. "I'd been getting close to that level but…I wanted him to win, you know? Having bred a horse that could win at that level made me feel legitimate. Real. I wasn't some crazy actress, not anymore. I was a real horse breeder."

She spoke calmly—no hysterics, no bravado. Just someone determined to prove her worth.

Yeah, he knew that feeling, too. Better than he wanted to.

"There are people in this world who don't know about that show," she said, staring at her phone. "People who only know me as Whitney Maddox, the breeder of Pride and Joy. You have no idea how *huge* that is."

"I'm starting to get one." He lifted the phone from her hand and studied the horse. He'd seen a similar shot to this one online. But she wasn't in either one.

She slid her fingertip over the screen and another horse came up. Even he could tell this was a younger one, gangly and awkward looking. "This is Joy's daughter, Ode to Joy. I own her mother, Prettier Than a Picture—Pretty for short. She was a world-champion dressage horse, but her owner got indicted and she was sold at auction. I was able to get her relatively cheap. She's turned out some amazing foals." The love in her voice was unmistakable. Pretty might have been a good business decision, but it was clear that the horse meant much more to Whitney than just a piece of property. "Ode's already been purchased," she went on. "I could keep studding Joy to Pretty for the rest of my life and find buyers."

"Sounds like job security."

"In another year, I'll deliver Ode," she went on. "She's only one right now." She flicked at her screen and another photo came up. "That's Fifi," she told him. "My rescued greyhound."

The sleek dog was sprawled out on a massive cushion on the floor, giving the camera a don't-bother-me look. "A greyhound?"

"I was fostering her and just decided to keep her," Whitney replied. "She'd run and run when she was younger and then suddenly her life stopped. I thought—and I know this sounds silly because she's just a dog—but I thought she understood me in a way that most other living creatures don't."

"Ah." He didn't know what else to say to that. He'd never felt much kinship with animals, not the way Phillip did with his horses. His father had never really loved the horses he'd bought, after all. They'd been only investments for him—investments that might pay off in money or prestige. "You foster dogs?"

She nodded enthusiastically. "The no-kill shelter in Bakersfield never has enough room." Her face darkened briefly. "At first they wouldn't let me take any animals but…" Her slim shoulders moved up and down. Then the cloud over her face was gone. "There's always another animal that needs a place to stay."

He stared at her. It could have been a naked play for pity—poor little celebrity, too notorious to be entrusted with animals no one else wanted. But that was not how it came out. "How many animals have you fostered?"

She shrugged again. "I've lost count." She flicked the screen again and a strange-looking animal appeared.

He held the phone up so he could get a better look, but the squished black-and-white face stayed the same. "What is *that*?"

"That," she replied with a giggle that drew his gaze to her face, "is Gater. He's a pug-terrier-something."

Hands down, that was the ugliest mutt Matthew had ever seen. "How long have you had him?"

"Just over two years. He thinks he rules the house. Oh, you should have seen him when Jo and Betty stayed with me. He was furious!" She laughed again, a sweet, carefree sound that did more to warm him than the sun ever could.

"What happened?"

"He bit Betty on the ankle, and she kicked him halfway across the living room. No broken bones or skin," she hurried to add. "Just a pissed-off dog and donkey. Gater thinks he's the boss, and Fifi doesn't care as long as Gater stays off her cushion."

Whitney leaned over and ran her fingers over the screen again. A photo of some cats popped up, but that was not what held Matthew's attention. Instead, it was the way she was almost leaning her head against his shoulder, almost pressing her body against his arm.

"That's Frankie and Valley, my barn cats."

"Frankie and Valley? Like Frankie Valli, the singer?"

"Yup." Without leaning away, she turned her face up toward his. Inches separated them. "Frankie was a…stray." Her words trailed off as she stared at Matthew's face, his lips. Her eyes sparkled as the blush spread over her cheeks like the sunrise after a long, cold night.

He could lean forward and kiss her. It'd be easy. For years, he'd thought about kissing Whitney Wildz. He'd been young and hormonal and trying so, *so* hard to be the Beaumont that his father wanted him to be. Fantasies about Whitney Wildz were a simple, no-mess way to escape the constant effort to be the son Hardwick Beaumont wanted.

Except he didn't want to kiss that fantasy girl anymore. He wanted to kiss the flesh-and-blood woman sitting next to him. She shouldn't attract him as she did. He should see nothing but a headache to be managed when he looked at her. But he didn't, damn it. He didn't.

Matthew couldn't help himself. He lifted the hand that

wasn't holding her phone and let the tips of his fingers trail down the side of her cheek.

Her breath caught, but she didn't turn away—didn't look away. Her skin was soft and warmed by the sun. He spread his fingers out until the whole of his palm cradled her cheek.

"I didn't realize you were such a fan of Frankie Valli," she said in a breathy voice. Her pupils widened as she took another deep breath. As if she was waiting for him to make his move.

"I'm not." The problem was, Matthew didn't have a move to make. Phillip might have once moved in on a pretty woman without a care in the world about who saw them or how it'd look in the media.

But Matthew cared. He had to. It was how he'd made a place for himself in this family. And he couldn't risk all of that just because he wanted to kiss Whitney Maddox.

So, as much as it hurt, he dropped his hand away from her face and looked back at the screen. Yes. There were cats on the screen. Named after an aging former pop idol.

He could still feel Whitney's skin under his touch, still see her bare back…

Something outside the window caught his eye. He looked up to see two women in their mid-twenties standing on the sidewalk in front of the restaurant. One had her phone pointed in their general direction. When they saw that he'd noticed them, they hurried along, giggling behind their hands.

Dread filled him. Okay, yes, Whitney was recognizable— but she wasn't the only woman in the world with an unusual hair color, for crying out loud. This had to be…a coincidence.

He turned his attention back to the phone, but pictures of cats and dogs and horses barely held his attention. He wanted their food to come so they could eat and get the hell out of here. He wanted to get Whitney to a place where even if people did recognize her, they had the decency not to make a huge deal out of it.

She flicked to the last photo, which was surprisingly *not* of an animal. Instead, it was of a cowgirl wearing a straw hat and tight jeans, one foot kicked up on a fence slat. The sun was angled so that the woman in the picture was bathed in a golden glow—alone. Perfect.

Whitney tried to grab the phone from him, but he held on to it, lifting it just out of her reach. "Is this...you?"

"May I have that back, please?" She sounded tense.

"It *is* you." He studied the photo a little more. "Who took it?"

"Jo did, when she was out last winter." She leaned into him, reaching for the phone. "Please."

He did as the lady asked. "So that's the real Whitney Maddox, then."

She froze, her fingertip hovering over the button that would turn the screen off. She looked down at the picture, a sense of vulnerability on her face. "Yes," she said in a quiet voice. "That's the real me." The screen went black.

He cleared his throat. "I think I like the real you."

Even then she didn't look at him, but he saw the smile that curved up her lips. "So," she said in a bright voice, "your turn."

Hell. What was he supposed to say? He looked away—and right at the same two women he'd seen earlier. Except now there were four of them. "Uh..."

"Oh, don't play coy with me," she said as she slipped her phone back into her jacket pocket. Then she nudged him with her shoulder. "The real you. Go."

This time, when the women outside caught him looking, they didn't hurry off and they sure didn't stop pointing their cameras. One was on her phone.

It was then that he noticed the noise. The restaurant had gone from humming to a hushed whisper. The carols over the sound system were loud and clear. He looked over his shoulder and was stunned to find that a good part of the restaurant was staring at them with wide eyes. Cell phones were out. People were snapping pictures, recording videos.

Oh, hell. This was about to become a PR nightmare. Worse—if people figured out who he was? And put two and two together? Nightmare didn't begin to cut what this was about to become.

"We need to leave."

The women outside were headed inside.

"Are you trying to get…out…?" Whitney saw the women, then glanced around. "Oh." Shame flooded her cheeks. She grabbed her sunglasses out of her bag and shoved them back onto her face. "Yes."

Sadly, the glasses did little to hide who she was. In fact, they gave her an even more glamorous air, totally befitting a big-name star.

Matthew fished a fifty out of his wallet and threw it on the counter, even though they weren't going to eat anything they'd ordered.

As they stood, the small group of women approached. "It's really you," one of the woman said. "It's really Whitney Wildz!"

The quiet bubble that had been building over the restaurant burst and suddenly people were out of their seats, crowding around him and Whitney and shoving camera phones in their faces.

"Is this your boyfriend?" someone demanded.

"Are you pregnant?" someone else shouted.

"Are you ever going to clean up your act?" That insult was shouted by a man.

Matthew was unexpectedly forced into the role of bouncer. He used his long arms to push people out of Whitney's way as they tried to walk the twelve feet to the door. It took several minutes before they were outside, but the crowd moved with them.

He had his arm around her shoulders, trying to shield her as he rushed for his car. With his long legs, he could have left half of these idiots behind, but Whitney was much shorter than he was. He was forced to go slow.

Someone grabbed Whitney's arm, shouting, "Why did you break Drako's heart?"

Matthew shoved and shoved hard. They were at his car, but people were pushing so much that he had trouble getting the passenger door open. "Get back," he snarled as he hip-checked a man trying to grab a lot more than Whitney's arm. "Back off."

He got the door open and basically shoved her inside, away from what had rapidly become a mob. He slammed the door shut, catching someone's finger. There was howling. He was feeling cruel enough that he was tempted to leave the finger in there, but that would be the worst sort of headline—Beaumont Heir Breaks Beer Drinker's Hand. So he opened the door just enough to pull the offending digit out and then slammed it shut again.

Whitney sat in the passenger seat, already buckled up. She stared straight ahead. She'd gotten her hat back on, but it was too late for that. The parts of her face that were visible were tight and blank.

Matthew stormed around to the driver's side. No one grabbed him, but several people were recording him. Great. Just freaking great.

He got in, fired up the engine on his Corvette Stingray and roared off. He was furious with the waitress—she'd probably called her girlfriends to tell them that Whitney Wildz was at her table. He was furious with the rest of the idiots, who'd descended into a mob in mere minutes.

And he was furious with himself. He was the Beaumont who always, always handled the press and the public. Image was everything and he'd just blown his image to hell and back. If those people hadn't recognized him from the get-go, it wouldn't take much online searching before they figured it out.

This was exactly what he hadn't wanted to happen—Whitney Wildz would turn this wedding and his message into a circus of epic proportions. Yeah, he'd been a jerk to her about it last night, but he'd also been right.

Even if she was a cowgirl who fostered puppies and adopted greyhounds, even if she was a respected horse breeder, even if she was *nothing* he'd expected in the best possible ways, it didn't change the perception. The perception was that Whitney Wildz was going to ruin this wedding.

And he wouldn't be able to control it. Any of it. Not the wedding, not the message—and not himself.

He was screwed.

Six

They drove in silence. Matthew took corners as if he were punishing them. Or her. She wasn't sure.

She wished she had the capacity to be surprised by what had happened at the restaurant, but she didn't. Not anymore. That exact scene had played out time and time again, and she couldn't even feel bad about it anymore.

Instead, all she felt was resigned. She'd known this was going to happen, after all. And if she was disappointed by how Matthew had reacted, well, that was merely the by-product of him confusing her.

She'd allowed herself to feel hopeful because, at least some of the time, Matthew liked her.

The real her.

She thought.

She had no idea where they were, where they were going, or if they were going there in a straight line. He might be taking the long way just in case any of those fans had managed to follow them.

"Are you all right?" he growled out as he pointed his sleek car toward what she thought was downtown Denver.

She wouldn't flinch at his angry tone. She'd learned a long time ago that a reaction—any reaction—would be twisted around. Best to be a placid statue. Although that hadn't always worked so well, either.

"I'm fine."

"Are you sure? That one guy—he *grabbed* you."

"Yes." Had that been the same man whose hand had gotten crushed in the door?

Even though she had her gaze locked forward, out of the corner of her eye she could see him turn and give her a look of disbelief. "And that doesn't piss you off?"

This time, she did wince. "No."

"Why the hell not? It pissed me off. People can't grab you like that."

Whitney exhaled carefully through her nose. This was the sort of thing that someone who had never been on the receiving end of the paparazzi might say. Normal people had personal space, personal boundaries that the rest of humanity agreed not to cross. You don't grab my butt, I won't have you arrested.

Those rules hadn't applied to her since the days after her show had been canceled. The day she'd bolted away from her mother's overprotective control.

"It's fine," she insisted again. "It's normal. I'm used to it."

"It's bullshit," he snapped. "And I won't stand by while a bunch of idiots take liberties with you. You're not some plaything for them to grope or insult."

She did turn to look at him then. He had a white-knuckle grip on the steering wheel as he glared at the traffic he was speeding around. He was serious.

She couldn't remember the last time someone hadn't just stood by and watched the media circus take her down.

Like the time she'd flashed the cameras. She hadn't had on any panties because the dress made no allowances for anything, the designer had said. Yeah, she'd been high at the time, but had anyone said, "Gee, Whitney, you might want to close your legs"? Had anyone tried to shield her from the cameras, as Matthew had just done, until she could get her skirt pulled down?

No. Not a single person had said anything. They'd just kept snapping pictures. And that next morning? One of the worst in her life.

He took another corner with squealing tires into a parking spot in front of a tall building. "We're here."

"Are you on my side?" she asked.

He slammed the car into Park, causing her to jerk forward. "What kind of question is that?"

"I mean…" Was he the kind of guy who would have told her she was flashing the cameras? Or the kind who would have gotten out of the way of the shot? "No one's ever tried to defend me from the crowds before."

Now it was his turn to look at her as if she were nuts. "No one?"

This wasn't coming out well. "Look, like you said—in the interest of transparency, I need to know if you're on my side or not. I'm not trying to mess up your message. I mean, you saw how it was." Suddenly, she was pleading. She didn't just want him on her side, watching her back—she *needed* him there. "All I did was take off my hat."

He gave her the strangest look. She didn't have a hope in heck of trying to guess what was going on behind his deep blue eyes.

"That's just the way it is," she told him, her voice dropping to a whisper. Every time she let her guard down—every time she thought she might be able to do something normal people did, like go out to lunch with a man who confused her in the best possible ways—this was always what would happen. "I—I wish it wasn't."

He didn't respond.

She couldn't look at him anymore. Really, she didn't expect anything else of him. He'd made his position clear. His duty was to his family and this wedding. She could respect that. She was nothing but a distraction.

A distraction he'd almost kissed in a crowded restaurant. So when he reached over and cupped her face in his hand, lifting it until she had no choice but to look at him, she was completely taken off guard. "I refuse to accept that this is 'just the way it is.' I *refuse* to." His voice—strong and confident and so close—did things to her that she barely recognized. "And you should, too."

Once, she'd tried to fight back, to reclaim her name and her life. She'd tried to lend her celebrity status to animal shelters. It'd gotten her nothing but years of horrible headlines paired with worse pictures. She hadn't done anything public since the last incident, over two years ago.

She looked into his eyes. If only he were on her side… "What I do doesn't matter and we both know it."

He gave her another one of those looks that walked the fine line between anger and disgust. "So what are you going to do about it?"

She glared at him. She couldn't get mad at those people— but him? She could release a little rage on him. After all, he'd been barely better than those people last night. "I'm not going to sit around and fume and mope about how I'm nothing but a *commodity* to people. I'm not going to sit around and feel bad that once upon a time I was young and stupid and crazy. And I'm not going to let anyone else sit around and feel bad for me. I'm not an object of your pity *or* derision. Because that's not who I am anymore."

If he was insulted by her mini tirade, he didn't show it. He didn't even let go of her. Instead, one corner of his mouth curled up into an amused grin.

"Derision, huh?" He was close now, leaning in.

"Yes."

That'd been last night. Right after she'd first fallen into his arms. After she'd dared to hope she might have a little Christmas romance. The memory made her even madder.

"So if you're going to ask me to drop out, just get on with it so I can tell you I already told Jo I would and she begged me not to because *you* invited a bunch of strangers to her wedding and she wants one friend standing next to her. Now, are you on my side or not?"

Because if he wasn't, he needed to stop touching her. She was tired of not knowing where she stood with him.

He blinked. "I won't let anyone treat you like that."

"Because it's bad for your message?"

His fingers pulled against her skin, lifting her face up. Closer to him. "Because you are *not* a commodity to me."

The air seemed to freeze in her lungs, making breathing impossible. He was going to kiss her. God, she wanted him to. Just as she'd wanted him to kiss her in the restaurant.

And see what had happened? She could still feel that man's hand on her butt.

As much as she wanted to kiss Matthew—to be kissed for the real her, not the fake one—she couldn't.

"I'm going to ruin the wedding." It was a simple statement of an unavoidable fact.

It worked. A shadow clouded his face, and he dropped his hand and looked away. "We're going to be late."

"Right." She didn't want to do this anymore, didn't want to be the reason the wedding went off script. She wanted to go back to her ranch—back where dogs and cats and horses and even Donald, the crazy old coot, didn't have any expectations about Whitney Wildz.

Matthew opened her door and held out his hand for her. She'd promised Jo. Until Jo told her she could quit, she couldn't. She wouldn't. That was that.

So she sucked it up, put her hand in Matthew's and stood.

He didn't let go of her, didn't step back. Instead, he held on tighter. "Are you sure you're okay?"

She put on a smile for him. She wouldn't be okay until she was safely back home, acres of land between her and the nearest human. Then she'd put her head down and get back to work. In a while—a few weeks, a few months—this wedding would be superseded by another celebrity or royal doing something "newsworthy." This would pass. She knew that now. She hadn't always known it, though.

"I'm fine," she lied. Then, because she couldn't lie and look at him, she stared up at the white building. "Where are we?" Because the sign said Hotel Monaco.

"The Veda spa is inside the hotel."

He still didn't let her go. He tucked her hand into the crook of his elbow, as if they'd walked out of 1908 or something. When she shot him a look, he said, "Practice."

Ah, yes. That whole walking-down-the-aisle thing.

So she put on her biggest, happiest smile and held an imaginary bouquet in front of her. She'd been an actress once, after all. She could fake it until she made it.

He chuckled in appreciation. "That's the spirit," he said, which made her feel immensely better. He handed his keys to a valet and they strode through the hotel lobby as if they owned the place.

"Mr. Beaumont! How wonderful to see you again." The receptionist at the front desk greeted them with a warm smile. Her gaze flicked over Whitney. "How can I help you today?"

"We're here for the spa, Janice," he said. "Thank you." As he guided Whitney down a hallway, she gave him a look. "What?"

Jealousy spiked through her. "You check into a hotel in your hometown in the middle of the day often? So often they know you by name?"

He pulled up right outside the salon door. "The Beaumonts have been using the hotel for a variety of purposes for years. The staff is exceedingly discreet. Chadwick used it for board meetings, but our father was…fond of using it for other purposes." Then he blushed. The pink color seemed out of place on his cheeks.

Ah—the father who sired countless numbers of children. She bit her tongue and said, "Yes?"

"Nothing," he said with more force than she expected. "The Beaumonts have a long business relationship with the hotel, that's all. I personally do not check into the rooms."

He opened the door to the spa. Another receptionist stood to greet them. "Mr. Beaumont," she said with a deferential bow of the head. "And this is—" she checked a tablet "—Ms. Maddox, correct?"

"Yes," Whitney said, feeling her shoulders straighten a bit more. If she could get through this as Ms. Maddox, that'd be great.

"This way. Rachel is ready for you."

They went back to a private room. Whitney hadn't been in a private salon room in a long time. "This is nice," she said as Matthew held the door open for her.

"And it better stay that way. Rachel," he said to the stylist with every color of red in her hair, "can you give me a moment? I have something I need to attend to."

"Of course, Mr. Beaumont." Rachel turned to face her. "Ms. Maddox, it's a delight to meet you."

Whitney tried not to giggle. A delight? Really? Still, this was a good test of her small-talk skills. At the wedding, she would be meeting a lot of people, after all. "A pleasure," she agreed.

She sat in the chair, and Rachel fluffed her hair several times. "Obviously, the bride will have her hair up," Rachel said. "Ms. Frances Beaumont has requested Veronica Lake waves, which will look amazing. Ms. Serena Beaumont will have a classic twist. You…" Her voice trailed off as she fingered Whitney's home-cut pixie.

"Don't have a lot to work with," Whitney said. "I know. I was thinking. Maybe we should take it blond."

Rachel gasped in horror. "What? Why?"

"She's not taking it blond," Matthew announced from the door as he strode in. He didn't look at Whitney—he was too busy scowling at his phone. But the order was explicit.

"Of course not," Rachel hurriedly agreed. "That would be the worst possible thing." She continued fluffing. "We could add in volume and extensions. Blond is out but colored strands are very hot right now."

Whitney cringed. Extensions? Volume? Colored streaks?

Why not just put her in a torn T-shirt emblazoned with the *Growing Up Wildz* logo and parade her down the street?

"Absolutely not," Matthew snapped. "We're going for a glamorous, classic look here."

If the stylist was offended by his attitude, she didn't show it. "Well," she said, working her fingers through Whitney's hair, "I can clean up the cut and then we can look at clips? Something bejeweled that matches the dresses?"

"Perfect," Matthew agreed.

"People will recognize me," Whitney reminded him, just because she felt as if she should have some say in her appearance. She glanced at the stylist, who had the decency to not stare. "Just like they did at the restaurant. If you won't let her dye it, at least get me a wig."

"No." But that was all he said as he continued to scowl at his phone.

"Why the heck *not*?"

He looked up at her, his eyes full of nothing but challenge. "Because you are beautiful the way you are. Don't let anyone take that away from you." Then his phone buzzed and he said, "Excuse me," and was gone.

Whitney sat there, stunned, as Rachel cleaned up her pixie cut.

Beautiful?

Was that how he thought of her?

Seven

This was going south on him. Fast. Matthew struggled to keep his cool. He'd learned a long time ago that losing his temper didn't solve anything. But he was getting close to losing it right now.

When the photo of him and Whitney, taken from the sidewalk while they sat inside the restaurant, had popped up on Instagram with the caption OMG WHITNEY WILDZ IN DENVER!?! he'd excused himself from the stylist's room so that he could be mad without upsetting Whitney. She'd had enough of that already.

He'd already reported the photo, but he knew this was just the beginning. And after years of cleaning up the messes his siblings and stepmothers had left behind, he also knew there was no way to stop it.

He was going to make an effort, though. Containment was half the battle. The other half? Distraction.

If he could bury the lead on Whitney under some other scandal…

He scanned the gossip sites, hoping that someone somewhere had done something so spectacularly stupid that no one would care about a former teen star having lunch.

Nothing. Of all the weeks for the rest of the world to be on its best behavior.

In the days of old—when he'd found himself faced with a crowd of paparazzi outside his apartment, demanding a reaction about his second stepmother's accusation that she'd caught Hardwick Beaumont in bed with his mistress in this very hotel—Matthew had relied on distraction.

He'd called Phillip, told him to make a scene and waited for the press to scamper off. It'd worked, too. Bailing Phillip out was worth it when Hardwick had called Matthew into his office and told him he'd done a nice job handling the situation.

"You're not mad at Phillip? Or…me?" Matthew had asked, so nervous he'd been on the verge of barfing. The only other times Hardwick had called Matthew into his office had been to demand to know why he couldn't be more like Chadwick.

Hardwick had gotten up and come around his desk to put his hands on Matthew's shoulders. Hardwick had been older then, less than five years from dying in the middle of a board meeting.

"Son," Hardwick had said with a look that could have been described only as fatherly on his face. It'd looked so unnatural on him. "When you control the press, you rule the world—that's how a Beaumont handles it."

Son. Matthew could count on both hands the number of times that Hardwick had used that term of affection. Matthew had finally, *finally* done something the old man had noticed. For the first time in his life, he'd felt like a Beaumont.

"You just keep looking out for the family," Hardwick had said. "Remember—control the press, rule the world."

Matthew had gotten very good at controlling the press—the traditional press. It was the one thing that *made* him a Beaumont.

But social media was a different beast, a many-headed hydra. You cut off one Instagram photo, another five popped up.

He couldn't rely on Phillip to cause a scene anymore, now that the man was clean and sober. Chadwick was out, as well—he didn't deal with the press beyond the controlled environment of interviews that Matthew prescreened for him.

Matthew stared at his phone. He could call his sister Frances, but she'd want to know why and how and details before she did anything. And once she found out that her former childhood idol Whitney Wildz was involved...

That left him one choice. He dialed his younger brother Byron.

"What'd I do now?" Byron said. He yawned, as if Matthew had woken him up at two in the afternoon.

"Nothing. Yet." There was silence on the other end of the line. "You *are* in Denver, right?"

"Got in this morning." Byron yawned again. "Hope you appreciate this. It's a damn long flight from Madrid."

"I need a favor."

"You mean beyond flying halfway around the world to watch Phillip marry some horse trainer?" Byron laughed.

Matthew gritted his teeth. Byron sounded just like Dad. "Yes. I need you to be newsworthy today."

"What'd Phillip do this time? I thought he was getting married."

"It's not Phillip."

Byron whistled. "What'd you get into?"

Matthew thought back to the photo he'd already reported. Whitney—sitting right next to him. Those people hadn't known who he was, but it wouldn't take long for someone to figure out that Whitney Wildz was "with" a Beaumont. "I just need a distraction. Can you help me out or not?"

This was wrong. All wrong. He was trying to prove that the Beaumont family was back on track, above scandal. He was trying to prove that he had complete control over the situation. And what was he doing?

Asking his brother to make a mess only days before the wedding...to protect Whitney.

What was he thinking?

He was thinking about the way her face had closed down the moment she realized people were staring, the way she sat in his car as if he were driving her to the gallows instead of a posh salon.

He was thinking about the way she kept offering to change her hair—to drop out—so that he could stay on message.

He was thinking how close he'd come to kissing her at that lunch counter.

"How big a distraction?"

"Don't kill anyone."

"Damn," Byron said with a good-natured chuckle. "You'll bail me out?"

"Yeah."

There was a pause that made Matthew worry. "Hey—did you invite Harper to the wedding?"

"Leon Harper, the banker who forced Chadwick to sell the Brewery?"

"Yeah," was the uninformative response. But then Byron added, "Did you invite him?"

"No, I didn't invite the man who hated Dad so much he took it out on all of us. Why?"

"I'll only help you out if you invite the whole Harper family."

"He has a *family*?" Matthew had had the displeasure of meeting Harper only a few times, at board meetings or other official Brewery functions. The man was a shark—no, that was unfair to sharks everywhere. The man was an eel, slippery and slimy and uglier than sin.

Plus, there was that whole thing about hating the Beaumonts enough to force the sale of the family business

"Are you serious? Why on God's green earth would you want Harper there?"

"Do you want me to make headlines for you or not?" Byron snapped.

"They can't come to the wedding—there's no room in the chapel. But I'll invite them to the reception." There would be plenty of room for a few extra people at the Mile High Station. And in a crowd of six hundred guests—many of whom were extremely famous—the odds of Harper running into a Beaumont, much less picking a fight with one, were slim. Matthew could risk it.

"Done. Don't worry, big brother—I've got a bone or two to pick now that I'm Stateside." Byron chuckled. "Can't believe you want me to stir up trouble. You, of all people."

"I have my reasons. Just try not to get a black eye," Matthew told him. "It'll look bad in the photos."

"Yeah? This reason got a name?"

The back of Matthew's neck burned. "Sure. And does the reason you ran off to Europe for a year have a name?"

"I was working," Byron snapped.

"That's what I'm doing here. Don't kill anyone."

"And no black eyes. Got it." Byron hung up.

Matthew sagged in relief. Byron had been in Europe for over a year. He claimed he'd been working in restaurants, but really—who could tell? All that Matthew knew was that Byron had caused one hell of a scene at a restaurant before winding up in Europe. There he'd kept his head down long enough to stay the heck out of the headlines. That'd been good enough for Matthew. One less mess he had to clean up.

This would work. He'd send out a short, boring press release announcing that Whitney Maddox, former star of *Growing Up Wildz* and close friend of the bride, was in Denver for the Beaumont wedding. The Beaumonts were pleased she would be in the wedding party. He'd leave it at that.

Then tonight Byron would go off the rails. Matthew was reasonably sure that his little brother wouldn't actually kill anyone, but he'd put the odds of a black eye at two to one. Either way, he was confident that Byron would do something that washed Whitney right out of the press's mind. Who cared about a former child star when the prodigal Beaumont had returned to raise hell at his brother's wedding?

"Mr. Beaumont?" Rachel, the stylist, opened the door and popped her head out. "We're ready for the big reveal."

"How'd she turn out?" Now that he had his distraction lined up, he could turn his attention back to Whitney. *All* of his attention.

Rachel winked at him. "I think you'll be pleased with the results."

Matthew walked into the private room. Whitney's back was to him. Her hair wasn't noticeably shorter, but it was shaped and sleek and soft-looking. A large rhinestone clip was fastened on one side, right over her white streak. He walked around to the front. Her eyes were closed. She hadn't seen yet.

God, she was beautiful. *Stunning.* The makeup artist had played up her porcelain complexion by going easy on the blush and heavy on the red lips. Instead of the smoky eye that Frances and Serena were going to wear, the artist had gone with a cat's-eye look.

"Whoa," he heard himself say. How could people look at this woman and only see Whitney Wildz?

Because the woman sitting in the chair in front of him was so much *more* than Whitney Wildz had ever been.

Whitney's nose wrinkled at him, but there was no missing the sweet little smile that curved up the corners of her mouth.

He was *going* to kiss her. Just as soon as they didn't have hairstylists and makeup artists hanging around, he was going to muss up that hair and smudge that lipstick and he wasn't going to feel bad about it at all.

"Ready, Ms. Maddox?" Rachel said. She spun Whitney's chair around and said, "Ta-da!"

Whitney blinked at her reflection, her pale eyes wide with shock.

Rachel's smile tensed. "Of course, it'll look better with the dress. And if you don't like it…"

"No, it's perfect," Matthew interrupted. "Exactly how I want her to look. Great job."

Whitney swallowed. "Perfect?" It came out as a whisper. He noticed her chest was rising and falling with increasing speed.

He knew what was happening. His sister Frances had always done the same thing when she'd been busted for sneaking around with the hired help. The shallow, fast breathing meant only one thing.

Whitney was about to freak out.

"If you could give us a moment," he said to the stylist.

"Is everything—?" Rachel asked, throwing a worried look back at Whitney as Matthew hurried the woman out of the room.

"It's perfect," Matthew reassured her as he shut the door in her face. Then he turned back to Whitney.

She'd come up out of the chair and was leaning into the mirror now. His mind put her back in her dress. "You're going to look amazing."

She started, as if she'd forgotten he was still there. Meeting his gaze in the mirror's reflection, she gave him a nervous grin. "I don't look like...*her* too much?"

Like Whitney Wildz.

He couldn't see anything of that ghost of the past in the woman before him—anything beyond a distinctive hair color. She *wasn't* Whitney Wildz—not to him. She was someone else—someone better.

Someone he liked.

Someone he'd defend, no matter what the cost.

He couldn't help it. He closed the distance between them and brushed the careful edge of her hairstyle away from her cheek. Then he tilted her head back to face him.

"You look like *you*," he assured her.

Her gaze searched his. The desperation was undisguised this time. He wanted to make her feel better, to let her know that he'd take care of her. He wouldn't throw her to the wolves or leave her hanging.

His lips brushed hers. Just a simple, reassuring kiss. A friendly kiss.

Yeah, right.

Except…she didn't close her eyes. He knew this because he didn't, either. She watched him kiss her. She didn't throw her arms around his neck and she didn't kiss him back. She just…watched.

So he stopped.

She was even paler now, practically a ghost with red lips as she stared at him with those huge eyes of hers.

Damn it. For once he'd let his emotions do the thinking for him and he'd screwed up.

"Whitney…"

"Knock-knock!" Rachel said in a perky voice as the door opened. "What did we decide?"

He ran the back of his hand over his mouth and then looked at Whitney. "I think she's perfect."

Eight

Matthew had been right. The staff at the hotel and spa were exceedingly discreet. There were no cameras or phones pointed at her when she walked out of the hotel. No one yelled her name as the valet pulled up with Matthew's car. Not a single person tried to grab her while the doorman opened her door and waited for her to get seated.

But Matthew had kissed her. Somehow, that made everything worse. And better.

She didn't know which. All she knew was that when he'd touched her—when he'd looked at her—and said she looked like herself, she'd wanted to kiss him and not kiss him and demand to know which "you" she looked like.

Which Whitney he thought he was kissing.

God, her brain was a muddled mess. She knew what to expect from the crowd at the restaurant. She did not know what to expect from Matthew Beaumont.

Except that he was probably going to keep confusing her.

Which he did almost immediately.

"I have the situation under control," he told her as they drove off for what she hoped was Jo and Phillip's farm. She couldn't take any more of this gadding about town. "I've done a press release announcing your involvement in the wedding."

"You're *announcing* I'm here? I thought that's what you wanted to avoid." She was feeling better now. Ridiculous, yes. But the sight of her in that mirror, looking like…well, like a Hollywood movie star, but a classic one, had short-circuited her brain. And then he'd kissed her.

"Trust me—after what happened at the restaurant, everyone knows you're here. There's no putting that genie back in the bottle."

"This does not make me feel better." She ran her hand over her hair. It felt much smoother than normal. She didn't feel normal right now.

"As I was saying," Matthew went on with a tense voice, "I've sent out a short, hopefully boring press release announcing that we're happy you're here. Then tonight my younger brother Byron will do something excessive and highly Beaumont-like."

"Wait, what?"

He didn't look at her—traffic was picking up—but his grin was hard to miss. "Byron's going to bury the lead. That's you."

"I—I don't understand. I thought you wanted the Beaumonts to stay *out* of the headlines." She was sure that he'd said something to that effect yesterday.

"I do. Byron was going to be newsworthy anyway. He flew off to Europe over a year ago and even I don't know why. This is just…building on that buzz."

She gave him a look. Was he serious?

He was.

"And it's the kind of situation I'm used to dealing with," he went on. "I can control this kind of press. I'm not going to let people manhandle you." He said it in such a serious tone that she was momentarily stunned.

"Why?"

"Why what?"

She swallowed, hoping she wouldn't trip over her words.

At least she was safely buckled in a car. The chances of her tripping over her feet were almost zero. "Why are you doing this for me?"

"Because it's the right thing to do."

She wanted to believe that. Desperately. But… "You're going to throw a Beaumont under the bus for me? You don't even know me."

"That's not true. And it's not throwing Byron under the bus if he willingly agrees. The situation is under control," he said again, as if it was a mantra.

She wasn't sure she believed that, no matter how many times he said it. "You don't even *know* me," she repeated. "Yesterday you wouldn't have just thrown me under the bus to stay on message—you would have backed the bus over me a few times for good measure."

"I know you breed award-winning horses, rescue dogs, name your cats after aging pop singers and will do anything for your friends, even if it puts you in the line of fire." He glanced over at her. "I know you prefer jeans and boots but that you can wear a dress as well as any woman I've ever seen. I know that once you were a rock star but now you're not."

Her cheeks warmed at the compliments, but then she realized what he'd said. Rock star? She'd played a rock star on television. Most people considered her an actress first—if they considered her a musician at all.

Unless… There was something going on here, something that she had to figure out right now. "You recognized me. Right away."

He didn't respond immediately, but she saw him grip the steering wheel even tighter. "Everyone recognizes you. You saw what happened at lunch today."

"Women recognize me," she clarified. "Who watched the show when they were kids."

"I'm sure they do." Did he sound tense? He did.

She was getting closer to that *something*. "Did you watch my show?"

"Frances did." He sounded as if he was talking through gritted teeth. "My younger sister."

"Did you watch it with her?"

The moment stretched long enough that he really didn't have to answer. He used to watch the show. He used to watch *her*. "Did you see me in concert? Is that why you called me a rock star?"

In response, he honked the horn and jerked the car across two lanes. "Stupid drivers," he muttered.

Normally, she wouldn't want to know. She didn't want people's version of her past to project onto her present. But she needed to know—was this the reason why he'd run so hot and cold with her?

"Matthew."

"Yes, okay? I used to watch your show with Frances and Byron. Frances, especially, was a huge fan. We never missed an episode. It was the only time when I could *make* time for them, make sure they didn't feel forgotten by the family. Our father had already moved on to another wife, another set of new children and another mistress. He never had time for them, for any of us. And I didn't want my brother and sister to grow up like I had. So I watched the show with them. Every single one of them. And then your concert tour came through Denver the week before their fifteenth birthday, so I got them front-row tickets and took them. Our father had forgotten it was their birthday, but I didn't."

She sat there, flabbergasted. Jo had said Hardwick Beaumont was a bastard of a man, but to not even remember your own kids' birthdays?

"And…and you were amazing, all right? I'd always wondered if you really did the singing and guitar on the show or if it was dubbed. But it was all you up on that stage. You put on a hell of a show." His voice trailed off, as if he was lost in the memory, impressed with her musical talents all over again. "I'd always…" He sighed heavily.

"What? You'd always *what*?"

"I'd always had a crush on you." His voice was quiet, as if he couldn't believe he was saying the words out loud. "Seeing you in person—seeing how talented you really were—only made it worse. But then the show got canceled and you went off the rails and I felt…stupid. Like I'd fallen for a lie. I'd let myself be tricked because you were so pretty and talented. I was in college by then—it really wasn't cool to crush on a teen star. And the headlines—every time you made headlines, I felt tricked all over again."

Okay, so how was she supposed to reply to *that*? *Gosh, I'm sorry I destroyed a part of your childhood? That I never had a childhood?*

She'd had people tell her they loved her before—had it shouted at her on sidewalks. Love letters that came through her agent—he forwarded them to her with the quarterly royalty checks. And she'd had more than a few people tell her how disappointed they were that she wasn't a proper role model, that she wasn't really a squeaky-clean rock star.

That she wasn't what they wanted her to be.

"You weren't— Last night…you weren't mad at me?"

He chuckled. It was not a happy sound. "No. I was mad at myself."

Why hadn't she seen it earlier? He'd had a crush on her. He might have even fancied himself in love with her.

No, not with her. With Whitney Wildz.

"But *you* kissed *me*."

True, it hadn't been a let's-get-naked kind of kiss, but that didn't change the basic facts. He'd told her she was beautiful at several important points throughout the day, gone out of his way to reassure her, listened to her talk about her pets and…kissed her anyway.

He scrubbed a hand through his hair, then took an exit off

the highway. It was several minutes before he spoke. "I did." He said it as though he still didn't believe it. "My apologies."

"You're apologizing? For the kiss? Was it that bad?"

Yeah, he'd sort of taken her by surprise—she'd been in a state of shock about her face—but that wasn't going to be *it*, was it? One strike and she was out of luck?

"You didn't kiss me back."

"Because I didn't know who you thought you were kissing." Point of fact, despite all the illuminating personal details he'd just revealed, she *still* didn't know who he'd thought he was kissing.

"You," he said simply. "I was kissing you."

She opened her mouth to ask, *Who?*

This was not the time for ambiguous personal pronouns. This was the time for clarity, by God. Because if he still thought he was kissing a rock star or an actress, she couldn't kiss him back. She just couldn't.

But if he was kissing a klutz who rescued puppies…

She didn't get the chance to ask for that vital clarification, because suddenly they were at the guard gate for Beaumont Farms. "Mr. Beaumont, Ms. Maddox," the guard said, waving them through.

Matthew took the road back to the house at what felt like a reckless speed. They whipped around corners so fast she had to hold on to the door handle. Then they were screeching to a halt in front of Phillip and Jo's house. The place was dark.

Whitney's head was spinning from more than just his driving. She couldn't look at him, so she stared at the empty-looking house. "Who am I? Who am I to you?"

Out of the corner of her eye, she saw his hands flex around the steering wheel. After today she wouldn't be surprised if he'd permanently bent it out of shape, what with all the white-knuckle gripping he'd been doing.

He didn't answer the question. Instead, he said, "Can I walk you inside?"

"All right."

They got out of the car. Matthew opened the door to the house for her and then stood to the side so she could enter first. She had to stop—it was dark and she didn't know where the light switches were located.

"Here." Matthew's voice was close to her ear as he reached around her. She stepped back—back into the wall.

He flipped the light on but he didn't move away from her. Instead, he stood there, staring down at her with something that looked a heck of a lot like hunger.

What did people do in this situation?

To hell with what other people did. What did *she* want to do?

She still wanted the same thing she'd wanted when she'd shown up here—a little Christmas fling to dip her toes back into the water of dating and relationships. She still wanted to feel sexy and pretty and, yes, graceful.

But the way that Matthew was looking down at her...there was something else there, something more than just a casual attraction that might lead to some really nice casual sex.

It scared her.

"I don't think they're home," he said, his voice husky.

"That's a shame," she replied. He'd made her feel pretty today, but right now? That hunger in his eyes?

She felt sexy. Desirable.

He wanted her.

She wanted to be wanted.

Just a Christmas fling. The maid of honor and the best man. Something that'd be short and sweet and so, *so* satisfying.

He hesitated. "Is it?"

"No." She turned until her back was against the wall.

His other arm came up beside her, trapping her in between them. "I'll stop. If you want me to."

She touched one of his cheeks. His eyelashes fluttered. But he hadn't answered her question.

He seemed to realize it. "I don't know what you are to me," he told her, the words coming out almost harsh. He leaned down and touched his forehead to hers. "But I know *who* you are."

This time, she knew the kiss wouldn't be the soft, gentle thing he'd pressed against her lips before. This time, it would be a kiss that consumed her.

She wanted to be consumed.

But he hadn't clarified anything, damn it. She put her hands on his chest and pushed just hard enough to stop him. Not hard enough to push him away. "Tell me, Matthew. Tell me who you're going to kiss."

Now both of his hands were cradling her face—pulling her up to him. "Whitney," he whispered. The length of his body pressed her back against the wall, strong and hard and everything she wanted it to be. "Whitney Maddox."

She didn't wait for him to kiss her. She kissed him first. She dug her fingers into the front of his sweater and hauled him down so she could take possession of his mouth, so she could offer up her own for him.

He groaned into her as she nipped at his lower lip. Then he took control of the kiss. His tongue swept into hers as his hands trailed down her cheeks, onto her neck and down her shoulders. Then he picked her up. The sudden change in altitude caused her to gasp.

"You need to be taller," he told her as he kissed along her cheek to her neck, her ear. His hands were flat against her bottom, boosting her to make up for the eight-inch height difference between them. Then he squeezed.

She had no choice. Her legs went around his waist, pulling him into her. She could feel his erection straining against his pants, pressing against her. She trembled, suddenly filled with a longing she couldn't ignore for a single second more.

Then his hips moved, rocking into hers. The pressure was intense—*he* was intense. Even though she had on jeans, she could feel the pads of his fingertips through the denim, squeezing her, pulling her apart.

His body rocked against hers, hitting the spot that sent the pressure spiraling up. She wanted to touch him, wanted to feel all the muscles that were holding her up as if she weighed nothing at all, but suddenly she had to hold on to him for dear life as he ground against her.

Her head fell back and bounced off the wall, but she didn't care—and she cared a whole lot less when Matthew started nipping at her neck, her collarbone. His hips flexed, driving him against her center again and again.

"Oh," she gasped. "Oh, Matthew."

"Do you like it," he growled against her chest.

"Yes."

"Louder." He thrust harder.

"Yes—*Oh!*" She gasped again—he was— She was going to—

He rocked against her again, in time with his teeth finding the spot between her shoulder and neck. He bit down and rubbed and—and—

"Oh yes, oh yes, *oh yes!*" she cried out as he pinned her back against the wall and held her up as she climaxed.

"Kiss me back," he told her, his forehead resting against hers. He was still cupping her bottom in his hands, but instead of the possessive squeezing, he was now massaging her. The sensation was just right. *He* was just right. "Always kiss me back."

So she kissed him, even as the climax ebbed and her body sagged in his arms. She kissed him with everything she had, everything she wanted.

Because she wanted everything. Especially a man who put her first.

"Tell me what you want," he said. Already his hips were

moving again, the pressure between her legs building. "I want this to be perfect for you. Tell me everything you want."

She cupped his cheeks in her hands. "Perfect?"

He gave her a look that started out as embarrassed but quickly became wicked. "Do you doubt me?"

After that orgasm? For heaven's sake, they were still fully clothed! What was he capable of when they were naked?

She grinned at him, feeling wicked in her own right. "Prove it."

Nine

"Oh, I'll prove it," Matthew told her. He hefted her up again. Then they were moving. He carried her through the house. He knew where they were going—his old room. If he didn't get all these clothes off them and bury himself in her body soon, he might just explode.

She wasn't helping. True, she didn't weigh very much and, since he was carrying her, she didn't trip or stumble into him. But the way she busied herself by scraping her teeth over his earlobe? He was going to lose it. Him, who was always in control of the situation. Of himself.

She'd stripped that control away from him the moment she'd walked into his life.

"This is my old room," he told her when they got to her door. He managed to get the door open. Then he kicked it shut.

Then he laid her out on the bed. Normally, he took his time with women. He was able to keep a part of himself back—keep a certain distance from what he was doing, what they were trying to do to him. Oh, they enjoyed it—he did, as well—but that level of emotional detachment was important somehow. He didn't know why. It just was.

Besides, being detached made it easier to make sure the women he was with were getting what they wanted from him.

But seeing Whitney on his old bed? Her hair was mussed now, her red lipstick smudged. She was no longer the perfect beauty he'd tentatively—yes, detachedly—kissed in the salon.

She was, however, his. His for right now. And he couldn't hold back.

He stripped off his coat while she tried to wriggle out of her jeans. Then, just as he had his sweater over his head, she kicked him in the stomach.

"Oof," he got out through clenched teeth. He stepped out of range and jerked the sweater the rest of the way off.

"Sorry! Oh, my gosh, I'm so sorry." Whitney lay on her back. She had one leg halfway out of her jeans, the other stuck around the ankle. "I didn't— I wasn't trying to— Oh, *damn*."

He caught the jeans, now practically inside out, and yanked them off her. Then he climbed onto the bed. Her blush was anything but pale or demure. An embarrassing red scorched her cheeks.

"I'm sorry," she whispered, looking as if she might start crying.

He straddled her bare legs as he pinned her wrists by her head. "None of that," he scolded her. "Nervous?"

She dropped her gaze and gave him a noncommittal shrug.

"Look at me," he told her. "Do you still want to do this?"

She didn't look. "I'm such a klutz. I'm sorry I kicked you."

"*Look* at me, Whitney," he ordered. When she didn't, he slid her wrists over her head so he could hold them with one hand and then he took her by the jaw and turned her face to his.

There was so much going on under the surface. She was trying to hide it by not looking at him, but he wasn't having any of it. "Apology accepted. Now forget it happened."

"But—"

He cut her off with a kiss, his hand sliding down her neck. "One of the things I like about you is that you get clumsy when you're nervous. It's cute."

Defiance flashed over her face. Good. "I don't want to be cute."

"What do you want?"

She sucked in a tiny breath—and was silent.

Oh, no, you don't, he thought. He snaked his hand down her front and then up under her sweater until he found her breast.

God, what a breast. Full and heavy and warm—and so responsive. Even through her bra, her nipple went to a stiff point as he teased her. "Is that what you want?"

She didn't answer. Not in words. But her breathing was faster now, and she'd tucked her lower lip into her mouth.

What control he had regained when she'd kicked him started to fray like a rope. He rolled her nipple between his finger and thumb. Her back arched into him, so he did it again, harder. "Is that what you want?"

She nodded.

"Say it," he told her. "Say it or I will tie you to this bed and *make* you say it."

The moment the words left his mouth, he wondered where they'd come from. He didn't just randomly tie people up. He wasn't into that kinky stuff. And when he'd dreamed of making it with Whitney Wildz, well, hell, back then, he hadn't even known people did that sort of thing.

But she didn't reply. Her eyes got huge and she was practically panting, but she didn't utter a word.

Then she licked her lips. And he lost his head.

Challenge accepted.

He let go of her breast and pulled her up, then peeled her sweater off her. The bra followed. She said nothing as he tore her clothes off, but when he kissed the side of her breast, when he let his tongue trace over her now-bare shoulder, she shuddered into him.

He couldn't stop whatever this was he'd started. He'd made her cry out in the entry hall. He'd make her do it again. He wrenched his tie off, then looped it around her wrists. Not tight—he didn't want to hurt her. But knowing her, she'd hit him in the nose with her elbow and nothing ruined some really hot sex like a bloody nose.

The tie secure around her wrists, he loosely knotted it to the headboard. Then he got off the bed.

Whitney Maddox was nude except for a thin pair of pale pink panties that looked so good against her skin. Her breasts were amazing—he wanted to bury his face in them and lick them until she cried his name over and over.

And she was tied to his bed.

Because she'd let him do that. Because she'd *wanted* him to do that.

He'd never been so excited in his life.

He stripped fast, pausing only long enough to get the condom out of his wallet. He rolled it on and then went to her. "I want to see all of you," he said, pulling her panties down. She started to lift her legs so he could get them off her ankles, but he held her feet down. "I'm in charge here, Whitney."

He trailed a finger down between her breasts, watching her shiver at his touch. Finally, *finally*, she spoke.

"I expect perfection."

"And that's what you'll get."

He climbed between her legs and stroked her body. She moaned, her head thrashing from side to side as he touched her.

He couldn't wait much longer. "You okay?" he asked. He wanted to be sure. They could play this little game about making her say it, but he also didn't want to hurt her. "If it's not okay, you tell me."

"This is okay. This is…" She tried to shift her hips closer to his dick. "Am I…am I sexy?"

"Oh, babe," he said. But he couldn't answer her, not in words. So he fit his body to hers and thrust in.

"Matthew!" she gasped in the same breathless way she'd cried his name in the hall.

"Yeah, louder," he ground out as he drove in harder.

"Matthew!" she cried again. Her legs tried to come off the bed, and she almost kneed him in the ribs.

"Oh, no, you don't," he told her as he grabbed her legs and tucked them up under his arms. Then he leaned down into her.

She was completely open to him, and he took advantage of that in every way he knew how—and a few he didn't even know he knew.

"Is this what you want?" he demanded over and over.

"Yes." Always, she said yes.

"Say it louder," he ordered her, riding her harder.

"Yes! Oh, Matthew—*yes!*"

There was nothing else but the moment between when he slid out of her body and drove back in. No thoughts of family or message or public image. Nothing but the woman beneath him, crying out his name again and again.

Suddenly her body tensed up around his. "Kiss me," she demanded. "Kiss me!"

"Kiss me back," he told her before he lowered his lips to hers.

Everything about her went tight as she kissed him. Then she fell back, panting heavily.

Matthew surrendered himself to her body. He couldn't fight it anymore.

Then he collapsed onto her chest. Her legs slid down his, holding him close. He knew he needed to get up—he didn't want to lose the condom—but there was something about holding her after what he'd done to her...

Jesus—had he really tied her up? Made her cry out his name? That was...something his father would have done.

"Can you untie me now?" she asked, sounding breathless and happy.

Focus, he told himself. So he sat back and undid the tie from the headboard. He'd really liked that tie, too, but he doubted it'd ever be the same.

He started to get out of bed to get cleaned up and dressed, but she sat up and tackle-hugged him so hard it almost hurt. But not quite. After he got over his momentary shock, he wrapped his arms around her.

"Thank you," she whispered. "It was…"

"Perfect?" He hoped so, for her sake.

At that, she leaned back and gave him the most suggestive smile he'd ever seen. He could take her again. He had another condom. He could loop his demolished tie back through the headboard and…

"I'm not sure. We might have to do it again later. Just to have a point of comparison, you understand." Then a shadow of doubt crossed her face. "If you wanted to," she hurried to add.

He pulled her back into his arms. "I'd like that. I'd like that a lot. You were amazing. Except for the kicking part."

She giggled, her chin tucked in the crook of his neck. He grabbed one of her wrists and kissed where he'd had it bound.

Then, from the floor, his phone chimed Phillip's text message chime.

And the weight of what he was supposed to be doing came crushing back down on him.

Why was he lolling away the afternoon in bed with Whitney? This was not the time to be tying people up, for crying out loud. He had a wedding to pull off—a family image to save.

An image that was going to be a whole hell of a lot harder to save when Byron got done with it.

Matthew had to keep the wheels from falling off. He had

to take care of the family. He had to prove he was one of them. A Beaumont.

Then Whitney kissed his jaw. "Do you need to go?"

"Yeah."

He didn't want to. He wanted to stay here, wrapped up with her. He wanted to say to hell with the wedding, the message—he didn't care. He'd done the best he could.

He cared about Whitney. He shouldn't—her old image was going to keep making headaches for him and it'd been only twenty-four hours since he'd met her.

But that didn't change things.

And yet it changed everything.

The phone chimed again. And again. Different chimes. It sounded as though Byron had pulled his stunt.

"I've got to go bail out Byron," he told her. "But I'll see you soon." He got off the bed, trashed the condom and got dressed as fast as he could. By now his phone sounded like a bell choir.

"When?" She sat on the bed, her knees tucked up under her chin. Except for the part where she was completely nude—or maybe because of it—there was an air of vulnerability about her.

"Lunch, tomorrow. You've got to choose where you want to have the bachelorette party. I'll take you to all the places I've scouted out." He picked up his phone. Jeez, that was a lot of messages in less than five minutes. "What a mess," he muttered at his phone. "I'll get you at eleven—that'll give you time with Jo and it'll give me time to fix this."

He leaned down and gave her a quick, hard kiss. Then he was out the door.

He knew he shouldn't be surprised that Phillip was standing in the living room—this was his house, after all—but the last thing Matthew needed right now was to be confronted by his brother.

Phillip looked at him with a raised eyebrow. But instead

of asking about Whitney, he said, "Byron got picked up. He said to tell you he's sorry, but the black eye was unavoidable."

Matthew's shoulders sagged. His little brother had done exactly what he wanted him to—but damned if it didn't feel as though Matthew was suddenly right back at the bottom of the very big mountain he was doomed to be constantly climbing—Mount Beaumont. "What'd he do?"

"He went to a restaurant, ordered dinner, asked to see the chef and proceeded to get into a fistfight with the man."

Matthew rubbed the bridge of his nose. "And?"

"The media is reporting he ordered the salmon."

"Ha-ha. Very funny. I'll get him."

He was halfway to the door when Phillip said, "Everything okay with Whitney?"

"Fine," he shot back as he picked up the pace. He had to get out of here, fast.

But Phillip was faster. He caught up to Matthew at the door. "Better than yesterday?"

"Yes. Now, if you'll excuse me…"

Phillip grinned. "Never thought you had it in you, man. You always went for such…boring women."

"I don't know what you're talking about."

Denial—whether it was to the press or his family—came easily to Matthew. He had years of practice, after all.

"Right, right." He gave Matthew the smile that Matthew had long ago learned to hate—the one that said *I'm better than you are*. "Just a tip, though—from one Beaumont to another—always wipe the lipstick off *before* you leave the bedroom."

Matthew froze. Then he scrubbed the back of his hand across his mouth. It came away bright red.

Whitney's lipstick.

"Uh…this isn't what it looks like."

"Really? Because it looks like you spent the afternoon sleeping with the maid of honor." Matthew's fists curled, but

Phillip threw up his hands in self-defense. "Whatever, man. I'm not about to throw stones at your glass house. Say," he went on in a too-casual voice, "this wouldn't have anything to do with Byron telling me he'd done what you asked him to, would it? Except for the black eye, of course."

Matthew moved before he realized what he was doing. He grabbed Phillip by the front of his shirt. "Do. Not. Give. Her. Crap."

"Dude!" Phillip said, trying to peel Matthew's hands away from his shirt. "Down, boy—down!"

"Promise me, Phillip. After all the messes I cleaned up for you—all the times I saved your ass—*promise me* that you won't torture that woman. Or Byron won't be the only one with a black eye at this wedding."

"Easy, man—I'm not going to do anything."

Matthew let go of his brother. "Sorry."

"No, you're not. Go." Phillip pushed him toward the door. "Bail Byron out so we can all line up for your perfect family wedding. That's what you want, isn't it?"

As Matthew drove off, his mind was a jumble of wedding stuff and family stuff and Whitney. Zipping Whitney into the bridesmaid dress. Stripping her out of her clothes. Admiring her perfectly done hair. Messing her hair up.

He had to pull this wedding off. He had to stay on message. He had to prove he belonged up there with the other Beaumonts, standing by Phillip's side.

That was what Matthew wanted.

Wasn't it?

Ten

She checked her watch. Three to eleven. She'd gotten up at her regular time and gone out with Jo to look at the young mare she was working with. Jo hadn't pressed her about Matthew, except to say, "You and Matthew…" there'd been a rather long pause, but Whitney hadn't jumped into the breach "…do all right yesterday?" Jo had finally finished.

"Yeah. I think you were right about him—he seems like a good guy who's wound a bit too tight."

Which *had* to be the explanation as to why he'd tied her to the bed with a necktie.

Which did nothing to explain why she'd let him do it and explained even less why she'd enjoyed it.

And now? Now she was going to spend the afternoon with him again. Which was great—because it'd been so long since she'd had sex with another person and Matthew wasn't just up to the task—he was easily the best lover she'd ever had.

But it was also nerve-racking. After all, he'd tied her to the bed and made her climax several times. How was she supposed to look him in the eye after that? Yes, she'd slept around a lot when she'd been an out-of-control teenager trying to prove she was an adult. Yes, she'd had some crazy sex. The gossips never let her forget that.

But she'd never had that kind of sex clean and sober. She'd never had any kind of sex sober. She'd never looked a lover in the eye without some sort of chemical aid to cover up her anxiety at what she'd done, what she might still do.

And now, as she adjusted her hat and sunglasses, she was going to have to do just that. She had no idea what to do next. At least she had Betty—the small donkey's ears were soft, and rubbing them helped Whitney keep some sort of hold on her anxiety. It would be fine, she kept telling herself as she petted Betty. *It* will *be fine.*

At exactly eleven, Matthew walked through the door at Phillip and Jo's house, cupped her face in his hands and made her forget everything except the way she'd felt beneath his hands, his body. Beautiful. Sexy.

Alive.

"Hi," he breathed as he rested his forehead against hers.

Maybe this wouldn't be complicated. It hadn't seemed complicated when he'd pinned her to the wall yesterday. Maybe it would be…easy. She grinned, slipping her arms around his waist. "Hi." Then she looked at him. "You're wearing a tie?"

Color touched his cheeks, but he didn't look embarrassed. If anything, he looked the way he had yesterday—hungry for more. Hungry for her.

"I usually wear ties." Heat flushed down her back and pooled low. But instead of pulling that tie off, he added, "Are you ready?"

She nodded, unable to push back against the anxiety. This time, at least, it didn't have anything to do with him. "We have to go, right?"

He leaned back and adjusted her hat, making sure her hair was fully tucked under it. "We'll just look at the places. And after yesterday, I cut a couple of the other options off the list, so it's only four places. We'll park, go in, look at the menu and come back out. Okay?"

"What about lunch?" Because the going-in part hadn't been the problem yesterday.

"I decided we'll have lunch at my apartment."

She looked at him in surprise. "You decided, huh?"

Thus far, she hadn't actually managed to successfully make it through a meal with him. If they were alone at his place, would they eat or...?

He ran his thumb over her lower lip. "I did." Then Betty butted against his legs, demanding that he pet her, too. "You getting ready to walk down the aisle, girl?" he asked as he checked his phone. "We need to get going."

Despite the kiss that followed this statement—how was she going to make it to lunch without ripping his clothes off?—by the time they got into the car and were heading off the farm, she was back to feeling uneasy. She didn't normally fall into bed with a man she'd known for a day. Not since she'd started over.

Matthew had said he knew she was Whitney Maddox... but had he, really? He'd admitted having a huge crush on her back in the day.

"You're nervous," he announced when they were back on the highway, heading toward Denver.

She couldn't deny it. At least she'd made it into the car without stepping on him or anything. But she couldn't bring herself to admit that she was nervous about him. So she went with the other thing that was bothering her. "How's your brother—Byron?"

Matthew exhaled heavily. "He's fine. I got him bailed out. Our lawyers are working to get the charges dropped. But his black eye won't be gone by the wedding, so I had to add him to the makeup artist's list."

"Oh." He sounded extremely put out by this situation, but she was pretty sure he'd told his brother to do something dramatic. To bury her lead. She couldn't help but feel that, at the heart of it, this was her fault.

"The media took the bait, though. You didn't even make the website for the *Denver Post*. Who could pass up the chance to dig up dirt on the Beaumont Prodigal Son Returned? That's the headline the *Post* went with this morning. It's already been picked up by *Gawker* and *TMZ*."

She felt even worse. That wasn't the message Matthew wanted. She was sure that this was exactly what he'd wanted to avoid.

"You're quiet again," he said. He reached over and rubbed her thigh. "This isn't your fault."

The touch was reassuring. "But you're off message. Byron getting arrested isn't rehabilitating the Beaumont family image."

"I know." He exhaled heavily again. "But I can fix this. It's what I do. There's no such thing as bad PR."

Okay, that was another question that she didn't have an answer to. "Why? Why is *that* what you do?"

Matthew pulled his hand back and started drumming his fingers against the steering wheel. "How much do you know about the Beaumonts?"

"Um…well, you guys were a family beer company until recently. And Jo told me your father had a bunch of different children with four different wives and he had a lot of mistresses. And he forgot about your sister and brother's birthday."

"Did Jo say anything else?"

"Just that you'd threatened all the ex-wives to be on their best behavior."

"I did, you know." He chuckled again, but there was at least a little humor in it this time. "I told them if they caused a scene, I'd make an example out of them. No one's hands are clean in this family. I've buried too many scandals." He shot her an all-knowing grin. "They won't risk pissing me off. They know what I could do to them."

She let that series of ominous statements sink in. Suddenly, she felt as if she was facing the man who'd caught her the first night—the man who'd bury her if he got the chance.

But that wasn't the man who'd made love to her last night—was it? Had he offered his brother up as bait to protect her...or because that was still an easier mess to clean up than the one she'd make?

"Are your hands clean?"

"What?"

"You said no one's hands in your family are clean. Does that include you?"

His jaw tensed, and he looked at her again. He didn't say it, but she could tell what he was thinking. Not anymore. Not since he tied her to the bed.

Just then his phone chimed. He glanced down at the screen before announcing, "We need to keep to the schedule."

Right. They weren't going to talk about him right now.

He obviously knew a great deal about her past, but what did she know about him? He was a Beaumont, but he was behind the scenes, keeping everyone on message and burying leads.

"We're here," he announced after a few more minutes of driving. She nodded and braced herself for the worst.

The restaurant seemed overdone—white walls, white chairs, white carpet and what was probably supposed to be avant-garde art done in shades of black on the wall. A white tree with white ornaments stood near the front. It was the most depressing Christmas tree Whitney had ever seen. If a restaurant was capable of trying too hard, this one was. Whitney knew that Jo would be miserable in a place like this.

"Seriously?" she whispered to Matthew after reading the menu. Most of it was in French. She had no idea what kind of food they served here, only that it would be snooty.

"One of the best restaurants in the state," he assured her. Then they went to a smaller restaurant with only six tables that had a menu full of locally grown microgreens and other items that Whitney wasn't entirely sure qualified as food. Honest to God, one of the items touted a kind of tree bark.

"How well do you even know Jo?" she asked Matthew as they sped away from the hipster spot. "I mean, really. She's a cowgirl, for crying out loud. She likes burgers and fries."

"It's a nice restaurant," he defended. "I've taken dates there."

"Oh? And you're still seeing those women, are you?"

Matthew shot her a comically mean look.

She giggled at him. This was nice. Comfortable. Plus, she hadn't had to take her hat or sunglasses off, so no one had even looked twice at her. "Gosh, maybe it was your pretentious taste in dining, huh?"

"Careful," he said, trying to sound serious. The grin, however, completely undermined him. "Or I'll get my revenge on you later."

All that glorious heat wrapped around the base of her spine, radiating outward. What was he offering? And more to the point—would she take him up on it this time?

Still, she didn't want to come off as naive. "Promises, promises. Do either of the remaining places serve real food?"

"One." His phone chimed again. "Hang on." He answered it. "Yes? Yes, we're on our way. Yes. That's correct. Thanks."

"*We're* on our way?"

That got her another grin, but this one was less humorous, hungrier. "You'll see."

After a few more minutes, they arrived at their destination. It wasn't so much a restaurant but a pub. Actually, that was its name—the Pub. Instead of the prissiness of the first two places, this was all warm wood and polished brass. "A bar?"

"A pub," he corrected her. "I know Jo doesn't drink, so I was trying to avoid places that had a bar feel to them. But if I left it up to Frances, she'd have you all down at a male strip club, shoving twenties into G-strings."

Realization smacked her upside the head. This wasn't about her or even Jo—this whole search for a place to have a bachelorette party was about managing his sister's image. "You were trying to put us in places that would look good in the society page."

His mouth opened, but then he shut it with a sheepish look. "You're right."

The hostess came forward. "Mr. Beaumont, one moment and I'll get your order."

"Wait, what?"

He turned to her and grinned. "I promised you lunch." He handed her a menu. "Here you go."

"But…you already ordered."

"For the bachelorette party," he said, tipping the menu toward her.

She looked it over. There were a few oddities— microgreens, again!—but although the burgers were touted as being locally raised and organic, they were still burgers. With fries.

"In the back," Matthew explained while they were waiting, "they have a more private room." He leaned down so that his mouth was right by her ear. "It's perfect, don't you think?"

Heat flushed her neck. She certainly hadn't expected Denver at Christmas to be this…warming. "You knew I was going to pick this place, didn't you?"

"Actually, I reserved rooms in all four restaurants. There'll be people looking to stalk the wedding party no matter what. And since we've been seen going over the menu at three of the places, they won't know where to start. This will throw them off the trail."

She gaped at him. *That* was what covering your bases looked like. She'd never been able to plan like that. Which was why she was never ready for the press.

"Really? I can't decide if that's the most paranoid thing I've ever heard or the most brilliant."

He grinned, brushing his fingers over her cheek. "You can't be too careful."

He was going to kiss her. In public. She, more than anyone, knew what a bad idea that was. But she was powerless to stop him, to pull away. Something about this man destroyed her common sense.

The hostess saved Whitney from herself. "Your order, Mr. Beaumont."

"Thank you. And we have the private room for Friday night?"

"Yes, Mr. Beaumont."

Matthew grabbed the bagged food. "Come on. My place isn't too far away."

Matthew pulled into the underground parking lot at the Acoma apartments. He'd guessed right about the Pub, which was a good feeling. And after Whitney's observations about burgers and fries, he felt even better about ordering her that for lunch.

But best of all was the feeling of taking Whitney to his apartment. He didn't bring women home very often. He'd had a couple of dates that turned out to be looking for a story to tell—and sell. Keeping his address private was an excellent way to make sure that he wouldn't get up in the morning and find paparazzi parked outside the building, ready to catch his date leaving his place in the same outfit she'd had on the night before.

He wasn't worried about that happening with Whitney. First off, he had no plans of keeping her here all night long—although that realization left him feeling strangely disappointed. But second?

As far as he could tell, no one had made him as the man sitting next to Whitney Wildz the other day. Frankly, he couldn't believe it—it wasn't as if he were an unknown quantity. He talked to the press and his face was more than recognizable as a Beaumont.

Still, it was a bit of grace he was willing to use as he led Whitney to the elevator that went up to the penthouse apartment.

Inside, he pressed her back against the wall and kissed her hungrily. Lunch could wait, right?

Then she moaned into his mouth, and his body responded. He'd wanted to do this since he'd walked into Phillip's house this morning—show her that he could be spontaneous, that he could give her more than just one afternoon. He wanted to show her that there was more to him than the Beaumont name.

Even as the thought crossed his mind, the unfamiliarity of it struck him as…wrong. Hadn't it *always* been about the Beaumont name?

"Oh, Matthew," she whispered against his skin.

Yeah, lunch could wait.

Then the doors opened. "Come on," he said, pulling her out of the elevator and into his penthouse.

He wanted to go directly to the bedroom—but Whitney pulled up short. "Wow. This is…perfect."

"Thanks." He let go of her long enough to set the lunch bag down on a counter. But before he could wrap his arms around her again, she'd walked farther in—not toward the floor-to-ceiling windows but toward the far side of the sitting room.

The one with his pictures.

As Whitney stared at the Wall of Accomplishments, as he thought of it, something Phillip had said last night came back to him. *You always went for such boring women.*

They hadn't been boring. They'd been *safe*. On paper, at least, they'd been perfect. Businesswomen who had no interest in marrying into the Beaumont fortune because they had their own money. Quiet women who had no interest in scoring an invite to the latest Beaumont Brewery blowout because they didn't drink beer.

Women who wouldn't make a splash in the society pages.

Whitney? She was already making waves in his life— waves he couldn't control. And he was enjoying it. Craving more. Craving *her*.

"This…" Whitney said, leaning up on her tiptoes to look at the large framed photo that was at the center of the Wall of Accomplishments. "This is a wedding photo."

Eleven

"Yes. That's my parents' wedding."

The tension in his voice was unmistakable.

"But you're in the picture. That's you, right? And the boy you're standing next to—that's Phillip? Is the other one Chadwick?" The confusion pushed back at the desire that was licking through her veins. She couldn't make sense out of what she was looking at.

"That's correct." He sounded as if he were confirming a news story.

"But...you're, like, five or something? You're a kid!"

A tight silence followed this statement. She might have crossed some line, but she didn't care. She was busy staring at the photo.

A man—Hardwick Beaumont—was in a very nice tuxedo. He stood next to a woman in an exceptionally poofy white dress that practically dripped crystals and pearls. She had giant teased red hair that wasn't contained at all by the headband that came to a V-point in the middle of her forehead. The look spoke volumes about the high style of the early '80s.

In front of them stood three boys, all in matching tuxedos. Hardwick had his hand on Chadwick's shoulder. Next to Chadwick stood a smaller boy with blond hair. He wore a wicked grin, like a sprite out to stir up trouble. And standing in front of the woman was Matthew. She had her hand on his shoulder as she beamed at the camera, but Matthew looked as though someone were jabbing him with a hatpin.

When he did speak, he asked, "You didn't know that I wasn't born a Beaumont?"

She turned to stare at him. "What? No—what does that mean?"

He nodded, nearly the same look on his face now that little-kid Matthew had worn for that picture. "Phillip is only six months older than I am."

"Really?"

He came to stand next to her, one arm around her waist. She leaned into him, enjoying this comfortable touch. Enjoying that he wasn't holding himself apart from her.

"It was a huge scandal at the time—even by Beaumont standards. My mother was his mistress while he was still married to Eliza—that's Phillip and Chadwick's mother." He paused, as if he were steeling himself to the truth. "Eliza didn't divorce him for another four years. I was born Matthew Billings."

"Wait—you didn't grow up with your dad?"

"Not until I was almost five. Eliza found out about me and divorced Hardwick. He kept custody of Chadwick and Phillip, married my mom and moved us into the Beaumont mansion."

She stared at him, then back at the small boy in the photo. *Matthew Billings.* "But you and Phillip seem so close. You're planning his wedding. I just thought…"

"That we'd grown up together? No." He laughed, a joyless noise. "I remember her telling me how I'd have my daddy and he'd love me, and I'd have some brothers who'd play with me, so I shouldn't be sad that we were leaving everything behind. She told me it was going to be perfect. Just…perfect."

The way he said it made it pretty clear that it wasn't. Was this why everything had to be *just so*? He'd spent his life chasing a dream of perfection?

"What happened?"

He snorted. "What do you think? Chadwick hated me—deeply and completely. Sometimes Phillip was nice to me because he was lonely, too." He pointed at the wedding photo. "Sometimes he and Chadwick would gang up on me because I wasn't a real Beaumont. Plus, my mom got pregnant with Frances and Byron almost immediately and once they were born…well, they were Beaumonts without question." He sighed.

His dad had forgotten about him. That was basically what Jo had said Hardwick Beaumont did—all those wives, mistresses and so many children that they didn't even know how many there were. What a legacy. "So how did you wind up as the one who takes care of everyone else?"

He moved, stepping back and wrapping both arms around her. "I had to prove I belonged—that I was a legitimate Beaumont, not a Billings." He lowered his head so that his lips rested against the base of her neck.

She would not let him distract her with something as simple, as perfect, as a kiss. Not when the key to understanding *why* was right in front of her.

"How did you do that?"

His arms were strong and warm around her as they pulled her back into his chest. All of his muscles pressed against her. and for a moment she wondered if he was going to push her against the wall and make her cry out his name again, just to avoid answering the question.

But then he said, "I copied Chadwick. I got all As, just like Chadwick did. I went to the same college, got the same MBA. I got a job at the Brewery, just like Chadwick. He was the perfect Beaumont—still is, in a lot of ways. I thought—It sounds stupid now, but I thought if I could just *be* the per-

fect Beaumont, my mom would stop crying in her closet and
we'd be a happy family."

"Did it work?" Although she already knew the answer
to that one.

"Not really." His arms tightened around her, and he
splayed his fingers over her ribs in an intimate touch. She
leaned into him, as if she could tell him that she was here
for him. That he didn't have to be perfect for her.

"When Frances and Byron were four, my parents got divorced. Mom tried to get custody of us, but without Beaumont money, she had nothing and Hardwick's lawyers were
ruthless. I was ten."

"Do you still see her?"

"Of course. She's my mother, after all. She works in a li-
brary now. It doesn't pay all of her bills, but she enjoys it. I
take care of everything else." He sighed against her skin, his
hands skimming over her waist. "She apologized once. Said
she was sorry she'd ruined my life by marrying my father."

"Do you feel the same way?"

He made a big show of looking around his stunning apartment. "I don't really think this qualifies as 'ruined,' do you?"

"It looks perfect," she agreed. But then, so did the wedding photo. One big happy family.

"Yeah, well, if there's one thing being a Beaumont has
taught me, it's that looks are everything. Like when a jealous
husband caught Dad with his wife. There was a scene—well,
that's putting it mildly. I was in college and walked out of
my apartment one morning and into this throng of reporters
and photographers and they were demanding a good reaction
quote from me—they wanted something juicy, you know?"

"I know." God, it was like reliving her own personal hell
all over again. She could see the paparazzi jostling for position, shouting horrible things.

"I didn't know anything about what had happened, so
I just started…making stuff up." He sounded as if he still

didn't believe he'd done that. "The photos had been doctored. People would do anything for attention, including lay a trap for the richest man in Denver—and we would be suing for libel. The family would support Hardwick because he was right. And the press—they took the bait. Swallowed it hook, line and sinker. I saved his image." His voice trailed off. "He was proud of me. He told me, 'That's how a Beaumont handles it.' Told me to keep taking care of the family and it'd be just fine."

"Was it?"

"Of course not. His third wife left him—but he bought her off. He always bought them off and kept custody of the kids because it was good for his image as a devoted family man who just had really lousy luck when it came to women. But I'd handled myself so well that when a position in the Brewery public relations department opened up, I got the job."

He'd gone to work for his brother after that unhappy childhood. She wasn't sure she could be that big of a person. "Do your brothers still hate you?"

He laughed. "Hell, no. I'm too valuable to them. I've gotten Phillip out of more trouble than he even remembers and Chadwick counts me as one of his most trusted advisors. I'm…" He swallowed. "I'm one of them now. A legitimate Beaumont—the brother of honor at the wedding, even. Not a bastard that married into the family five years too late." He nuzzled at the base of her neck. "I just… I wish I'd known it would all work out when I was a kid, you know?"

She knew. She still wished she knew it would all work out. Somehow. "You know what I was doing when I was five?"

"What?"

"Auditions. My mother was dragging me to tryouts for commercials," she whispered into the silence. "I didn't care about acting. I just wanted to ride horses and color, but she wanted me to be famous. *She* wanted to be famous."

She'd never understood what Jade Maddox got out of it,

putting Whitney in front of all those people so she could pretend she was someone else. Hadn't just being herself been enough for her mother?

But the answer had been no. Always no. "My first real part was on *Larry the Llama*—remember that show? I was Lulu."

Behind her, Matthew stilled. Then, suddenly, he was laughing. The joy spilled out of him and surrounded her, making her smile with him. "You were on the llama show? That show was terrible!"

"Oh, I know it. Llamas are *weird*. Apparently everyone agreed because it was canceled about six months later. I'd hoped that was the end of my mother's ambitions. But it wasn't. I *dreamed* about having brothers or sisters. I didn't even meet my dad until I became famous, and then he just asked for money. Jade's the one who pushed me to audition for *Growing Up Wildz*, who pushed them to make the character's name Whitney."

His eyebrows jumped. "It wasn't supposed to be Whitney?"

"Wendy." She gave him a little grin. "It was supposed to be Wendy Wildz."

"Wow. That's just…" he chuckled. "That's just wrong. Sorry."

"It is. And I went along with it. I thought it'd be cool to have the same name as the character. I had no idea then it'd be the biggest mistake of my life—that I'd never be able to get away from Whitney Wildz."

He spun her around and gazed into her eyes. "That's not who you are to me. You know that, right?"

She did know. She was pretty sure, anyway. "Yes."

But then his mouth crooked back into a smile. "But… Lulu?"

"Hey, it was a great show about a talking llama!" she shot

back, unable to fight back the giggle. "Are you criticizing quality children's programming written by adults on drugs?"

"What was it ol' Larry used to say? 'It's Llama Time!' And then he'd spit?" He tried to tickle her.

She grabbed his hands. "Are you mocking llamas? They're majestic animals!"

He tested her grip, but she didn't let go. Suddenly, he wasn't laughing anymore and she wasn't, either.

She found herself staring at his tie. It was light purple today, with lime-green paisley amoebas swimming around on it. Somehow, it looked good with the bright blue shirt he was wearing. Maybe that was because he was wearing it.

He leaned down, letting his lips brush over her forehead, her cheek. "What are you going to do?" he asked, his voice husky. "Tie me up? For making fun of a llama?"

Could she *do* that? It'd been one thing to let him bind her wrists in a silk necktie yesterday. He'd been in control then—because she'd wanted him to be. She'd wanted him to make the decisions. She'd wanted to be consumed.

But today was different. She didn't want to be consumed. She wanted to do the consuming.

She pushed him back and grabbed his tie, then hauled his face down to hers. "I won't stand for you disparaging llamas."

"We could sit." He nodded toward a huge dining-room table, complete with twelve very available chairs surrounding it. The chairs had high backs and latticed slats. But he didn't pull his tie away from her hand, didn't try to touch her. "If you want to."

"Oh, I want to, mister. No one gets away with trash-talking *Larry the Llama*." She jerked on his tie and led him toward the closest chair.

"Larry was ridiculous," Matthew said as she pushed him down.

"You're going to regret saying that." She yanked his tie

off. It still had the knot in it, but she didn't want to stop to undo it. She didn't want to stop and think about what she was doing.

"Will I?" He held his hands behind his back.

"Oh, you will." She had no idea how to tie a man up in the best of times. So she looped the tie around his wrists and tried to tie it to the slat that was at the correct height. "There. That'll teach you."

"Will it?" Matthew replied. "Llamas look like they borrowed their necks from gira—"

She kissed him, hard. He shifted, as if he wanted to touch her, but she'd tied him to a chair.

She could do whatever she wanted, and he couldn't stop her.

Sexy. Beautiful. Desirable. That was what she wanted.

She stepped away from him and began to strip. Not like yesterday, when she'd been trying to get out of her clothes so fast she'd kicked him. No, this time—at a safe distance—she began to remove her clothing slowly.

First she peeled her sweater over her head, then she started undoing the buttons on her denim shirt—slowly. One at a time.

Matthew didn't say anything, not even to disparage llamas.

Instead, Matthew's gaze was fastened to Whitney's fingertips as one button after another gave.

A look of disappointment blotted out the desire when he saw the plain white tank top underneath.

"It's cold here," she told him. "You're supposed to dress in layers when it's cold."

"Did the llamas tell you that? They lie. You should be naked. Right now."

She was halfway through removing her tank top when he said that. She went ahead and pulled it the rest of the way off, but said, "Just for that, I'm not going to get naked."

His eyes widened in shock. "What?"

She stuck her hands on her hips, which had the handy effect of thrusting her breasts forward. "And you can't touch me, because you're tied up." Just saying it out loud gave her a little thrill of power.

For too damn long, she'd felt powerless. The only way she'd been able to control her own life was to become a hermit, basically—just her and the animals and crazy Donald up the valley. People took what they wanted from her—including deciding who she was—and they never gave her any say in the matter.

Not Matthew. He'd let her do whatever she wanted—be whoever she wanted.

She could be herself—klutzy and concerned about her animals—and he still looked at her with that hunger in his eyes.

She kicked off her boots and undid her jeans. Miracle of miracles, she managed to slide them off without tipping over and falling onto the floor.

Matthew's eyes lit up with want. With *need*. She could see him breathing faster now, leaning forward as if he could touch her. Heat flooded her body—almost enough to make up for the near-nudity. She felt sexy. Except for the socks.

Well, she'd already told him she wasn't going to get naked. Although she was having a little trouble remembering why, exactly.

Plus, he was sitting there fully clothed. And she didn't know where any condoms were. "Condoms?" They were required. She'd been accused of being falsely pregnant far too many times to actually risk a real pregnancy. The last thing she needed in her life were more headlines asking, Wildz Baby Daddy?

"Wallet." The tension in his voice set her pulse racing. "Left side."

"You just want me to touch you, don't you?"

He grinned. "That is the general idea. Since you won't let me touch you."

"I stand for llama solidarity," she replied as she walked toward him. "And until you can see reason…"

"Oh, I can't. No reason at all. Llamas are nature's mistake."

"Then you'll just have to stay tied up." She straddled him, but she didn't rest her weight on his obvious erection. Instead, she slid her hands over his waist and down around to his backside until she felt his wallet. She fished it out, dropped it onto the table and then ran her hands over him again. "I didn't really get to feel all of this last time," she told him.

"You were a little tied up."

She ran her hands over his shoulders, down his pecs, feeling the muscles that were barely contained by the button-down shirt and cashmere sweater. Then she leaned back so she could slide her hands down and feel what was behind those tweed slacks.

Matthew sucked in a breath so hot she felt it scorch her cheek as she touched the length of his erection. He leaned forward and tried to kiss her, but she pulled away, keeping just out of his reach. "Llama hater," she hissed at him.

"You're killing me," he ground out as he tried to thrust against her hand.

"Ah-ah-ah," she scolded. This was…*amazing*. She knew that, if he wanted to, he could probably get out of the tie and wrap her in his arms and take what she was teasing him with. And she'd let him because, all silliness aside, she wanted him *so* much.

But he wasn't. He wouldn't, because she was in control. She had all the power here.

Tension coiled around the base of her spine, tightening her muscles beyond a level that was comfortable. She let her body fall against his, let the contact between them grow.

"Woman," Matthew groaned.

She tsked him as she slid off. "You act like you've never been tied up before."

"I haven't." His gaze was fastened to her body again. She felt bold enough to strike a pose, which drew another low groan from him.

"You…haven't?"

"No. Never tied anyone up before, either." He managed to drag his gaze up to her face. "Have you?"

"No." She looked at him, trying to keep her cool. He hadn't done this before? But he'd seemed so sure of himself last night. It wasn't as though she expected a man as hot and skilled as he was to be virginal, but there was something about being the first woman he'd wrapped his necktie around—something about her being the first woman he'd let tie him to a chair—that changed things.

No. No! This was just a little fling! Just her dipping her sexual toes back in the sexy waters! This was not about developing new, deeper feelings for Matthew Beaumont!

She snagged the condom off the table. "I demand an apology on behalf of Larry the Llama and llamas everywhere." Then—just because she could—she dropped the condom and bent over to pick it up.

He sucked in another breath at the sight she was giving him. "I beg of your forgiveness, Ms. Maddox." She shifted. *"Please,"* he added, sounding desperate. "Please forgive me. I'll never impugn the honor of llamas again."

Ms. Maddox.

She needed him. Now.

She slid her panties off but kept the bra on. She undid his trousers and got them down far enough that she could roll the condom on. Then, unable to wait any longer, she let her body fall onto his.

She grabbed his face and held it so she could look into his eyes. "Matthew…"

But he was driving up into her and she was grinding down onto him and there wasn't time for more words. They had so very little time to begin with.

"Want to...kiss you," Matthew got out, each word punctuated with another thrust.

His clothing was rubbing against her, warming her bare skin. Warming everything. "Kiss me back?" she asked, knowing what the answer would be.

"Always," he replied as she lowered her lips to his. "Always."

Always. Not just right now but always.

She came apart when their lips met, and he came with her.

She lay on top of him, feeling the climax ebb from her body. It was then that she wished she hadn't tied him up, because she wanted him to hold her.

"I had no idea that llamas got you so worked up," he told her as his lips trailed over her bare shoulder. "I'll make a mental note of it."

She leaned back and grinned at him. "Was that okay? I didn't hurt you or anything—? Oh! I should untie you!"

"Uh—wait—" he said, but she was already at the back of the chair.

The tie lay in a heap on the ground. Not around his wrists. Not tied to the chair. She blinked at the puddle of bright fabric. Confusion swamped her. "When— Wait—if you weren't tied up, why didn't you touch me?"

He stood and adjusted his pants before turning around. He was, for all intents and purposes, the same as he'd been before, minus one necktie. And she was standing here in her socks and a bra. She couldn't even tie a man up.

"Why didn't you touch me?" she asked again.

He came to her then, wrapping his arms around her and holding her tight to him. "Because," he said, his lips pressing against her forehead, "you tied me up. It was kind of like...making a promise, that you were in charge. I keep my promises."

"Oh," she breathed. People didn't often keep promises, not to her. Her mother hadn't protected her, hadn't managed

her money. Her former fiancé hadn't kept a single promise to her.

She had crazy Donald, who didn't know who she was, and…Jo, who'd promised that she wouldn't tell anyone about the months she'd spent with Whitney, wouldn't tell a living soul where Whitney lived.

And now Matthew was promising to follow her wishes.

She didn't know what to make of this.

From somewhere far away, his phone chimed. "Our lunch is probably ice-cold," he said without letting her go or answering his phone.

At the mention of the word *cold,* she shivered. She was mostly naked, after all. "We haven't had a successful meal yet."

The phone chimed again. It seemed louder—more insistent. "I need to deal with some things. But if you want to hang out for a bit, I can take you home and we can try to have dinner out at the farm?"

"I'd like that."

"Yeah," he agreed, brushing his lips over hers as his phone chimed again and again. "So would I."

Twelve

It was a hell of a mess. And what made it worse was that it was self-inflicted. He'd made this bed. Now he had to lie in it.

Matthew tried to focus on defusing the situation—which wasn't easy, given that Whitney was exploring his apartment. Normally, he didn't mind showing off his place. It was opulent by any normal standard—truly befitting a Beaumont.

But now? What would she see when she looked at his custom decorating scheme? Would she see the very best that money could buy or...would she see something else?

None of the other women he'd brought back here had ever focused on his parents' wedding picture. They might have made a passing comment about how cute he was as a kid, but the other women always wanted to know what it was like being Phillip's brother or meeting this actor or that singer. They wanted to know how awesome it was to be one of the famous Beaumont men.

Not Whitney. She already knew what fame felt like. And she'd walked away from it. She didn't need it. She didn't need other people's approval.

What must she think of him, that he *did* need it? That he had to have the trappings of wealth and power—that he had to prove he was not just *a* Beaumont but the best one?

Focus. He had a job to do—a job that paid for the apartment and the cars and, yes, the ties. Matthew didn't know why Byron had gone after that chef. His gut told him there was a history there, but he didn't know what it was and Byron wasn't talking.

So Matthew did what he always did. He massaged the truth.

He lied.

The other guy had swung first. All Byron had done was complain about an underdone salmon steak, and the chef took it personally. Byron was merely defending himself. So what if that wasn't what the police report said? As long as Matthew kept repeating his version of events—and questioning the motives of anyone who disagreed with him—sooner or later, his reality would replace the true events.

"What's in here?" Whitney called out. Normally, he didn't like people in general and women in particular to explore his space on their own. He kept his apartment spotless, so it wasn't that. He liked to explain how he'd decided on the decorating scheme, why the Italian marble was really the only choice, how a television that large was really worth it. He liked to manage the message of his apartment.

He liked to manage the people in his apartment.

However, Whitney was being so damned adorable he couldn't help but smile.

"Where?" he shouted back.

"Here— Oh! That's a *really* big TV!"

He chuckled. "You're in the theater room!"

"Wow…" Her voice trailed off.

He knew that in another five minutes they'd have almost the exact same conversation all over again.

Matthew realized he was humming as he gave his official Beaumont response to the "unfortunate" situation again and again. Byron was merely noting his displeasure with an undercooked dish. The Beaumonts were glad the cops were called so they could get this mess straightened out. They would have their day in court.

Then a new email popped up—this one wasn't from a journalist but from Harper, his father's nemesis.

"Thank you for inviting us to the reception of Phillip Beaumont and bride at the last second, but sadly, no one in the Harper family has the least interest in celebrating such an occasion."

The old goat hadn't even bothered to sign the kiss-off. Nice.

Normally, it would have bothered Matthew. Maybe it did, a little. But then Whitney called out, "You have your own gym? Really?"

And just like that, Matthew didn't care about Harper.

"Really!" he called back. He sent off a short reply stating how very much Harper would be missed—Hardwick Beaumont had always counted him as a friend. Which was another bold-faced lie—the two men had hated each other from the moment Hardwick had seduced Harper's first wife less than a month after Harper had married her. But Harper wasn't the only one who could write a kiss-off.

Speaking of kissing…Matthew checked the weather, closed his computer and went looking for Whitney. She was standing in his bathroom, of all places, staring at the wide-open shower and the in-set tub. "It's just you, right? Even the bathroom is monster huge!"

"Just me. You need to make a decision."

Her eyes grew wide. "About what?"

He brushed his fingers through her hair. It'd gotten mussed up when she'd stripped for him. He liked it better that way. "The weather might turn later tonight. If you want to go back to the farm, we'll need to leave soon."

One corner of her mouth curved up. "*If*? What's the other option?"

"You are more than welcome to stay here with me." He looked around his bathroom. "I have plenty of room. And

then I could show you how the shower works. And the bath."
He'd like to see that—her body wet as he soaped her up.

She gave him a look that was part innocence, part sheer
seduction. A look that said she might like to be soaped up—
but the thought scared her, as well. "I don't have any of my
things…"

He nodded in agreement. Besides, he tried to reason with
himself, just because there hadn't been paparazzi waiting for
them when they got to the building didn't mean that there
wouldn't be people out there in the morning. And the last
thing he needed right now was someone to see him and the
former Whitney Wildz doing the walk of shame.

"Besides," she went on, looking surprisingly stern, "it's
Christmas—almost, anyway—and you don't even have a
tree. Why don't you have a tree? I mean, this place is amazing—but no tree? Not a single decoration? Really?"

He brushed his fingertips over her cheeks again. He didn't
normally celebrate Christmas here. "I spend Christmas night
with my mom. If they're in town, Frances and Byron come
by. She always has stockings filled with cheesy gifts like
yo-yos and mixes for party dips. She has a small tree and
a roasted turkey breast and boxed mashed potatoes—not
high cuisine by any stretch." He wouldn't dare admit that
to anyone else.

Christmas night was the one night of the year when he
didn't feel like Matthew Beaumont. Back in Mom's small
apartment, cluttered with photos of him and her and Frances and Byron—but never Hardwick Beaumont—Matthew
felt almost as if he were still Matthew Billings.

It was a glimpse into the past—one that he occasionally let himself get nostalgic about, but it never lasted very
long. Then, after he gave his mother the present he'd picked
out for her—something that she could use but a nicer version than she could afford herself—he'd kiss her goodbye
and come back to this world. His world. The world where
he would never admit to being Matthew Billings. Not even
for an afternoon.

Except he'd just admitted it to Whitney. And instead of the clawing defensiveness he usually felt whenever anyone brought up the Billings name, he felt...lighter.

Whitney gave him a scolding look. "It sounds lovely. I watch *It's a Wonderful Life* and share a ham with Gater and Fifi. I usually bring carrots to the horses, that sort of thing." She sighed, leaning into his arms. "I miss having someone to celebrate with. That's why I came to this wedding. I mean, I came for Jo, but..."

"Tell you what—we'll head back to the farm now, because it looks all Christmassy, and then—" his mouth was moving before he realized what he was saying "—then after the wedding, maybe we can spend part of Christmas together before you go home?"

"I'd like that." Her cheeks flushed with warmth. "But I don't have a present for you."

He couldn't resist. "You are the only present I want. Maybe even tied up with a bow...." He gathered her into his arms and pressed her back against the tiled wall with a rather heated kiss.

Several minutes passed before she was able to ask, "Are you done with your work?"

"For now, yes." Later he'd have to log back in and launch another round of damage control. But he could take a few hours to focus on Whitney. "Let me take you home."

She giggled. "I don't think I have much of a choice in that, do I? My truck's still out on the farm." A look of concern crossed her face. "Can you drive your car in the snow?"

"I'm a Beaumont," he said, his words echoing off the tiled walls of the bathroom. "I have more than one vehicle."

After a comfortable drive out to the farm in his Jeep, Whitney asked him if he'd stay for dinner. Jo had already set a place for him at the table and Phillip said, "Hang out, dude."

So, after a quick check of his messages to make sure that

nothing else had blown up, Matthew sat down to dinner—homemade fried chicken and mashed potatoes. Finally, over easy conversation about horses and celebrities, he and Whitney managed to successfully eat a meal together.

Then Jo said, "We're going to watch *Elf*, if you want to join us."

"I auditioned for that movie," Whitney said, leaning into him. "But I was, um, under the influence at the time and blew it pretty badly, so Zooey Deschanel got the part. It's still a really funny movie. I watch it every year."

Matthew looked at Phillip, who was pointedly not smiling at the way Matthew had wrapped his arm around Whitney's waist. "Sure," Matthew heard himself say. "It sounds like fun."

As the women popped popcorn and made hot chocolate, of all things, Phillip pulled him aside under the pretense of discussing the sound for the movie. "Who are you," he said under his breath, "and what have you done with my brother Matthew?"

"Shove it," Matthew whispered back. He didn't want to have this conversation. Not even with Phillip.

His brother did no such shoving. "Correct me if I'm wrong," he went on, "but weren't you on the verge of personally throwing her out of the wedding a few nights ago?"

"Shove. It."

"And yesterday—well, she's an attractive woman. I can't fault you for sleeping with her. But today?" Phillip shook his head, clearly enjoying himself. "Man, I don't think I've ever seen you be so…lovey-dovey."

Matthew sighed. He wanted to deck Phillip so badly, but the wedding was in a matter of days. "Lovey-dovey?"

"Affectionate. I can't remember the last time I've seen you touch a woman, outside of handshakes and photo ops. And you *never* just sit around and watch a movie. You're always working."

"I'll have to log back on in a few hours. I'm still working."

Phillip looked at him out of the corner of his eye. "You can't keep your hands off her."

Matthew shrugged, hoping he looked noncommittal. He touched women. He took lovers. He was a Beaumont—having affairs was his birthright.

Boring women, he remembered Phillip calling them yesterday. Women he took to stuffy restaurants and to their own place to bed them so no one would see that he'd had a guest overnight.

It wasn't that he wasn't affectionate. It was that he was careful. He had to be.

He wished Jo and Whitney would hurry the hell up with that popcorn. "I like her."

"Which her? The fallen star or the horse breeder?"

"The horse breeder. I like her."

Phillip clapped him on the shoulder. "Good answer, man. Good answer. The movie is ready, ladies," he added as Jo and Whitney made their way over to them.

Matthew hurried to take the full mugs of cocoa—complete with marshmallows—from Whitney. Then Jo produced blankets. She and Phillip curled up on one couch with the donkey sitting at their feet as they munched popcorn and laughed at the movie.

Which left him and Whitney with the other couch. He didn't give a rat's ass for the popcorn. He set his cocoa down where he could reach it, then patted the couch next to him. Whitney curled up against his side and pulled the blankets over them.

"Do you watch a lot of movies?" he asked in a quiet voice, his mouth against her ear.

"I do. I get up really early when it's warm—farmer's hours—and I'm pretty tired at night. Sometimes I read—I like romances." He could see the blush over her face when she said that, as if he'd begrudge her a happy ending. "It took a while before I could watch things like this and not think a bunch of what-ifs, you know?"

He wrapped his arms around her waist and lifted her onto his lap. Maybe Phillip was right. Maybe he wasn't normally affectionate with the women who came into his life. But he *had* to touch Whitney.

They watched the movie. Whitney and Jo had clearly watched it together before. They laughed and quoted the lines at each other and had little inside jokes. Matthew's phone buzzed a few times during the show, but he ignored it.

Phillip was right about one thing—when was the last time he'd taken a night off and just hung out? It'd been a while. Matthew tried to think—had he planned on taking a couple of days off after the wedding? No, not really. The wedding was the unofficial launch of Percheron Drafts, Chadwick's new craft beer. Matthew had a 30 percent stake in the company. They were building up to a big launch just in time for the Big Game in February. The push was going to be hard.

He'd made plans to have dinner with his mother. That was all the time he'd originally allotted for the holiday. But now? He could take a few days off. He didn't know when Whitney was heading back to California, but if she wanted to stick around, he would make time for her.

By the time the movie ended, he and Whitney were lying down, spooning under their blankets. He hadn't had any popcorn, and the cocoa was cold, but he didn't care. With her backside pressed against him, he was having a hard time thinking. Other things were also getting hard.

But there was a closeness that he hadn't anticipated. He liked just holding her.

"I should go," he said in her ear.

She sighed. "I wish you didn't have to."

Phillip and Jo managed to get untangled from their covers first. "Uh, Matthew?"

"Yeah?" He managed to push himself up into a sitting position without dumping Whitney on the floor.

"Icy."

"You see what?"

"No, icy—as in ice. On your car. And the driveways."

"Damn, really?" He waited long enough for Whitney to sit up. Then he walked to a window. Phillip was right. A glaze of ice coated everything. "The weather said snow. Not ice. Damn. I should have…"

"You're stuck out here, man." Phillip gave him a playful punch in the shoulder. "I know it'll be a real hardship, but you can't drive home on ice."

Matthew looked at Whitney. She'd come to stand next to him. "Ice…wow," she said in the same tone she'd used when she'd been exploring his apartment. "We don't get ice out in California. Not like this!" She slipped her hand into his and squeezed.

He could stay the night. One night wrapped up in Whitney and then he could fall asleep with her in his arms. Wake up with her there, too. He didn't do that often. Okay, he didn't ever do that.

Only one problem. "I didn't bring anything."

"We have guest supplies," Jo called out.

Phillip stood up straight and looked Matthew over. "Yeah, we probably still wear the same size."

"Stay," Whitney said in a voice that was meant only for him. "Stay with me. Just for the night. Call it…an early Christmas present."

It really wasn't an argument. He couldn't drive home on ice and honestly? He didn't want to. Suddenly he understood why Phillip had always preferred the farmhouse. It was warm and lived-in. If Matthew went back to his apartment—monster huge, as Whitney had noted, and completely devoid of holiday cheer—and Whitney wasn't there with him, the place would feel…empty.

Lonely.

It'd never bothered him before. But tonight he knew it would.

"I'll need to log on," he told everyone. "We still have a wedding to deal with."

"Of course," Jo said. She was smiling, but not at him. At Whitney. "You do what you need to do."

Matthew spent an hour answering the messages he'd ignored. Whitney had gone up to read so she wouldn't distract him from his work. He knew he was rushing, but the thought of her in his room again—well, that was enough to make a man hurry the hell up.

When he opened his door, the fire was blazing in the hearth, and Whitney was in bed. She looked...perfect. He couldn't even see Whitney Wildz when he looked at her anymore. She was just Whitney.

The woman he wanted. "I was waiting for you," she told him.

"I'll make it worth the wait." Then she lifted up the covers and he saw that she was nude.

Thank God for ice.

Thirteen

The day of the bachelorette party came fast. Whitney got to stay on the farm for a couple of days, which should have made her happy. She was able to work with Jo and some of the many horses on the farm—Appaloosas, Percherons and Sun, the Akhal-Teke. Phillip treated her like a close friend and the staff on the farm was the definition of discreet and polite at all times. They made cookies and watched holiday shows. Even the farm manager, an old hand named Richard, took to calling her Whit.

By all rights, it should have been everything she wanted. Quiet. Peaceful. Just her and a few friends and a bunch of horses. No cameras, no gossips, no anything having to do with Whitney Wildz. Except...

She missed Matthew.

And that wasn't like her. She didn't miss people. She didn't get close enough to people to miss them when they went.

Well, that wasn't true. She'd missed the easy friendship with Jo when Jo had hitched her trailer back up to her truck and driven on to the next job.

But now, after only two days without him, she missed Matthew. And she shouldn't. She just shouldn't. So he'd made love to her that night, rolling her onto her stomach to do things to her that *still* made her shiver with desire when she thought about them. And so she'd woken up in his arms the next morning and they'd made love so sweetly that she still couldn't believe she hadn't dreamed the whole thing.

How long had it been since she'd woken up with a man in bed? A long time. Even longer since the man in question had made love to her. Told her how beautiful she was, how good she was. How glad he was that he'd stayed with her.

It was a problem. A huge one. This was still a temporary thing, a Christmas fling that would end with the toss of the bridal bouquet. If she were lucky, she'd get Christmas morning with him. And that'd be it. If she missed Matthew now, after just a couple of good days, how bad off would she be when she went home? When she wouldn't have to wait another day to see him?

How much would she miss him when she wasn't going to see him again?

It'd hurt to watch him get into his car and slowly drive away. He'd offered to let her come with him, but she'd refused. She was here for Jo and, anyway, Matthew had things he needed to do. Weddings to manage, PR debacles to control. Just another reminder of how far apart their lives really were.

To her credit, Jo hadn't said much about the sudden relationship. Just, "Are you having a good time with Matthew?"

"I am," Whitney had said truthfully. Although *fun* seemed as if it wasn't strong enough of a word. Fun was a lovely day at an amusement park. Being with Matthew? It was amazing. That was all there was to it. He was *amazing*.

"Good." That was all Jo said about it.

Now, however, Whitney and Jo were driving in to the Pub to meet the other women in the wedding party. Matthew would be out with Phillip and all their brothers—bowling, of all things. Although Whitney wasn't sure if that was one of those fake activities Matthew had planned to keep the paparazzi guessing.

Whitney kept her hat on as the hostess showed them back to the private room. There were already several other women there, as well as a small buffet laid out with salads, burgers and fries. *Matthew*, Whitney thought with a smile as she took off her hat and sunglasses. Maybe he did know Jo better than she thought.

"Hi, all," Jo said. "Let me introduce—"

"*Oh, my God*, it's really you! You're Whitney Wildz!" A young woman with bright red hair came rushing up to Whitney. In the brief second before she grabbed Whitney by the shoulders, Whitney could see the unmistakable resemblance to both Matthew and Phillip—but especially Matthew. The red hair helped.

"You really *are* here! And you know Jo! *How* do you know Jo? I'm Frances Beaumont, by the way."

"Hi," Whitney tried out. She'd known this was going to happen—and today was certainly a more controlled situation than normal. She had Jo and there were only a few women in the room. But she'd never really mastered the proper response to rabid fans.

"Yes, as I was saying," Jo said in a firm voice as she pried Frances's hands off Whitney's shoulders, "this is Whitney Maddox. She's a horse breeder. I know her because we've worked horses together." She tried to steer Frances away from Whitney, but it didn't work.

"You're really *here*. Oh, my God, I know you probably have this happen all the time, but I was your *biggest* fan. I loved your show *so* much and one time Matthew took me to see you in concert." Before Whitney could dodge out of the way, Frances threw her arms around her and pulled Whitney into a massive hug. "I'm *so* glad to meet you. You have no idea."

"Um…" was all Whitney could get out as her lungs were crushed. Frances was surprisingly strong for her size. "I'm getting one."

"Frances," Jo said, the warning in her voice unmistakable. "Could you at least let Whitney get her coat off before you embarrass yourself and go all fangirl?"

"Right, right! Sorry!" Frances finally let go. "I'm just so excited!" She pulled out her cell phone. "Can I get a picture? Please?"

"Um…" Whitney looked around, but she found no help. Jo looked pissed and the other women were waiting for her to make a decision. She was on her own here. What would Matthew do? He'd manage the message.

"If you promise not to post it on social media until after the wedding." She smiled at how in control that sounded.

"Of course! I don't have to post it at all—this is just for me. You have *no* idea how awesome this is." She slung her arm around Whitney's shoulders and held the camera up overhead before snapping the selfie. "That is so awesome," she repeated as she approved the picture. "Can I send it to Byron and Matthew? We always used to watch your show together."

"I've already met him. Matthew, that is." Suddenly, she was blushing in an entirely different way. And there was no hiding from it, since everyone in the room was staring at her.

Another woman stood up. "You'll have to excuse Frannie," this woman said with a warm smile. She looked nothing like a Beaumont, but beyond that, she was holding a small baby that couldn't be more than a month old. "She's easily excitable. I'm Serena Beaumont, Chadwick's wife. It's delightful to meet you." She shifted the baby onto her shoulder and held out a hand.

"Whitney." She didn't have a lot of experience dealing with babies, but it had to be safer than another hug attack from Frances. "How old is your baby?"

"Six weeks." Serena smiled. She turned so that Jo and Whitney could see the tiny baby's face. "This is Catherine Beaumont."

"She's adorable." She was actually kind of wrinkly and still asleep, but Whitney had no other points of reference, so the baby was adorable by default.

"Her being pregnant made getting the bridesmaids' dresses a mess," Frances said with a dramatic roll of her eyes. "Such a pain."

"Said the woman who is not now, nor has ever been, pregnant," Serena said. But instead of backbiting, the whole conversation was one of gentle teasing. The women were clearly comfortable with each other.

Whitney was introduced to the rest of the women in attendance. There was Lucy Beaumont, a young woman with white-blond hair who did not seem exactly thrilled to be at the party. She left shortly after the introductions, claiming she had a migraine.

Whitney also met Toni Beaumont, who seemed almost as nervous as Whitney felt. "Toni's going to be singing a song at the wedding," Jo explained. "She's got a beautiful voice."

Toni blushed, looking even more awkward. She was considerably younger than the other Beaumonts Whitney had met. Whitney had to wonder if she was one of Hardwick Beaumont's last children? If so, did that make her...maybe twenty? She didn't get the chance to find out. Toni, too, bailed on the proceedings pretty quickly.

Then it was just Jo, Frances, Serena and Whitney—and a baby who was sleeping through the whole thing. "They seem...nice," Whitney ventured.

"Lucy doesn't really like us," Frances explained over the lip of her beer. She was the only one drinking. "Which happens in this family. Every time Dad married a new wife, the new one would bad-mouth the others. That's why Toni isn't comfortable around us, either. Her mom told her we were all out to get her."

"And," Serena added, giving Frances a sharp look, "if I understand correctly, you *were* out to get her when you were a kid."

Frances laughed. "Maybe," she said with a twinkle in her eye. "There might have been some incidents. But that was more between Lucy and Toni. I was too old to play with *babies* by that point. Besides, do you know how much crap Phillip used to give me? I swear, he'd put me on the meanest horse he could find just to watch me get bucked off and cry. But I showed him," she told Whitney. "I learned how to stay on and I don't cry."

Serena rolled her eyes and looked at Whitney. "It's a strange family."

Whitney nodded and smiled as if it were all good fun, but she remembered Matthew telling her how his older brothers used to blame him for, well, *everything*.

"Okay, yeah," Frances protested. "So we're all a little nuts. I mean, I'm never going to get married, not after having *that* many evil stepmothers. Never going to happen. But that's the legacy we were born into as Beaumonts—all except Matthew. He's the only one who was ever nice to all of us. That's why Lucy and Toni were here today—he asked them to come. Said it was important to the family, so they came. The only person who doesn't listen to him is Eliza, Chadwick and Phillip's mom. Everyone else does what he says. And seriously? That man not only wouldn't let me take you guys to the hottest club, but he wouldn't even let me hire a stripper." She scoffed while rolling her eyes, a practiced gesture of frustration. "He can be such a control freak. He probably even picked out your shoes or something."

There was a pause, and then both Frances and Serena turned to look at Whitney.

Heat flooded Whitney's cheeks. Matthew had, in fact, picked out her shoes. And her hairstyle. And her lipstick. Right before he'd mussed them all up. She wasn't about to argue the control-freak part. But then, he'd also let her tie him up. He'd kept up the illusion even though her knot hadn't held. Just so she could be in control.

"So," Frances said in a too-bright tone. "You *have* met Matthew."

"Yes." The one word seemed safer. She wasn't used to kissing and telling. Heck, she was still getting used to the kissing thing. She was absolutely not going to tell anyone about it.

"And?" Frances looked as if she were a lioness about to pounce on a wounded wildebeest.

Whitney hated being the wildebeest. "We're just working to make sure that the wedding goes smoothly. No distractions." She thought it best not to mention the shoes. Or the ties.

Serena nodded in appreciation, but Frances made a face of exasperation. "Seriously? He's had a huge crush on you for, like, forever! I bet he can barely keep his hands off you. And frankly, that man could stand to get distracted."

"Frannie!" Jo and Serena said at the same time. The baby startled and began to mew in tiny-baby cries.

"Sorry," Serena said, draping a blanket over her shoulder so she could nurse, Whitney guessed.

"Well, it's true! He's been driving us all nuts with this wedding, insisting it has to be perfect. Honestly," Frances said, turning her attention back to Whitney, "I'm not sure he ever just does something for fun. It'd be good for him, you know?"

Whitney was so warm she was on the verge of sweating. She thought of the way he'd ignored his phone while they cuddled on the couch, watching a Christmas movie. Was that fun?

"He had a crush on Whitney Wildz," she explained, hoping her face wasn't achieving a near-fatal level of blush. "That's not who I am."

They'd cleared that up before the clothes had started to come off. He knew that she was Whitney Maddox. He liked her for being her, not because she'd once played someone famous. End of discussion.

Except…Matthew was, in fact, having trouble keeping his hands off her. Off *her*, right? Not Whitney Wildz?

She didn't want the doubt that crept in with Frances's knowing smile. But there it was anyway. She couldn't be 100 percent sure that Matthew wasn't sleeping with Whitney Wildz, could she? Just because he'd called her Ms. Maddox a few times—was that really all the proof she needed?

"Sure," Frances said with a dismissive wave of her hand. "Of course."

"You're being obnoxious," Serena said. Then she added to Whitney, "Frances is good at that."

"I'm just being honest. Matthew's way too focused on making sure we all do what he thinks we should. This is a rare opportunity for him to do something for himself. Lord knows the man needs more fun in his life. You two should go out." She paused, a smile that looked way too familiar on her face. "If you haven't already."

This was it. After all these years, all those headlines and horrible pictures and vicious, untrue rumors, Whitney was finally going to die of actual embarrassment. She'd have thought she couldn't feel it this much anymore—that she was immune to it—but no. All it took was one affair with a Beaumont and an "honest" conversation with his little sister and *boom*. It was all over.

Jo sighed. "Are you done?"

"Maybe," Frances replied, looking quite pleased with herself.

"Because you know what Matthew's going to do to you when he finds out you're treating my best friend like this, don't you?"

At that, a look of concern managed to blot out Frances's satisfied smile. "Well…hey, I've been on my best behavior ever since you guys decided to get married. No headlines, no trouble. I leave that to Byron."

And Byron had gotten into trouble only because Matthew had asked him to. For her. There was a moment of silence, during which Whitney considered getting her coat and going. Except she couldn't leave without Jo. Damn it.

Then the silence was broken. "But what about—?" Serena said, joining the fray.

"Or the one time when you—" added Jo.

"Hey!" Frances yelped, her cheeks turning almost as red as her hair. "That's not fair!"

"We're just being honest," Serena said with a grin that bordered on mean.

Jo nodded in agreement, giving Whitney an encouraging grin. "What did Phillip tell me about that one guy? What did he call you? His Little Red—"

Frances's phone chimed. "Sorry, can't listen to you make fun of me. Must answer this very important text!" She read her message. "Byron says he can't believe that's really Whitney Wildz." She began to type a reply.

"What are you going to tell him?" Whitney asked.

"What do you think?" Frances winked at her. "That your name is Whitney Maddox."

"Is that…Whitney Wildz?" Byron held his phone up to his good eye. "Seriously?"

"What?" Matthew grabbed the phone away from his brother. "Jesus." It was, in fact, Whitney, standing next to Frances, smiling for the camera. She looked good. A little worried but that was probably because Frances had a death grip on her shoulders.

He was going to kill both of them. Why would Whitney let anyone take her picture? And hadn't he warned Frances not to do anything stupid? And didn't taking a picture of Whitney and plastering it all over the internet count as stupid?

The phone chimed as another message popped up.

Tell Matthew that she made me promise to only send it to you. No social media.

Matthew exhaled in relief. That was a smart compromise. He could only hope Frances would hold up her end of that promise. He handed the phone back over, hoping he appeared nonchalant. "That was a character she played," he said in his most diplomatic tone. "Her name is Whitney Maddox." He shot a look at Phillip, who was enjoying a cigar on Matthew's private deck.

Phillip gave him his best innocent face, then mimed locking his lips and throwing away the key.

The guys had managed to arrive at Matthew's place without notice. It was just the five of them. Byron didn't get along with their other half brothers David and Johnny at all and Mark was off at college. Matthew had decided to keep the guest list to the wedding party. Just the four Beaumont men who could tolerate each other. Most of the time.

Plus the sober coach, Dale. When Phillip was out on the farm, he was fine, but he'd been sober for only seven months now and with the pressure of the wedding, no one wanted a relapse. Hands down, that would be the worst thing to happen to the wedding. There would be no recovering from that blow to the Beaumont image and there would be no burying that lead. It would be game over.

Matthew and Phillip had made sure that Dale would be available for any event that took place away from the farm. Currently, Dale was sitting next to Phillip, talking horses. This was what the Beaumont men had come to—soda and cigars on a Saturday night. So this was what getting old was like.

"Who?" Chadwick asked, taking the phone.

"Whitney Wildz." Byron was studying the picture. "She was this squeaky-clean girl who starred in a rock-and-roll update of *The Partridge Family* called *Growing Up Wildz.* Man," he went on, "she looks *amazing.* Do you know if she's—?"

"She's not available," Matthew said before he could stop himself. But Byron was a Beaumont. There was no way Matthew wanted his little brother to get it into his head that Whitney was fair game.

All three of his brothers gave him a surprised look. Well, Chadwick and Byron gave him a look. Phillip was trying too hard not to laugh, the rat bastard. "I mean, if anyone tried to hit on her, it'd be a media firestorm. Hands off."

"Wait," Chadwick said, studying the picture again. "Isn't this the woman who's always stoned or flashing the camera?"

"She's not like that," Matthew snapped.

"What Matthew means to say," Phillip added, "is that in real life, Whitney raises prize-winning horses and lives a fairly quiet life. She's definitely *not* a fame monster."

"*This* is the woman who's the maid of honor?" Chadwick's voice was getting louder as he glared at the phone. "How is this Whitney Wild person not going to make this wedding into a spectacle? You know this is the soft opening for Percheron Drafts, Matthew. We can't afford to have anything compromise the reception."

"Hey—easy, now, Chad." Chadwick flinched at Phillip's nickname for him. Which Phillip used only when he was trying to piss off the oldest Beaumont. Yeah, this little bachelor party was going downhill, fast. "It's going to be fine. She's a friend of Jo's and she's not going to make a spectacle of anything. She's perfectly fine. Matthew was worried, too, but he's seen that she's just a regular woman. Right?" He turned to Matthew. "Back me up here."

"Phillip's correct. Whitney will be able to fulfill her role in the wedding with class and style." *And*, he added mentally, *with a little luck, some grace*. He hoped he'd put her in the right shoes. "She won't be a distraction. She'll help demonstrate that the Beaumonts are back on top."

Funny how a few days ago he'd been right where Chadwick was—convinced that a former star would take advantage of the limelight that went with a Beaumont Christmas wedding and burn them all. Now all Matthew was worried about was Whitney getting down the aisle without tripping.

He glanced up to see Byron staring at him. "What?"

It was Chadwick who spoke first. "We can't afford any *more* distractions," he said, half punching Byron on the arm. "I'm serious."

"Fine, fine. I prefer to eat my own cooking anyway." Byron walked off to lean against the railing on the balcony. Then he looked back at Matthew.

Matthew knew what that meant. Byron wanted to talk. So he joined his little brother. Then he waited. It was only when Phillip distracted Chadwick by asking about his baby daughter that Matthew said, "Yes?"

"Did you ask Harper?" Byron kept his voice low. Yeah, there was no need to let Chadwick in on this conversation. If Chadwick knew that they'd asked his nemesis to the wedding... Well, Matthew hated bailing people out.

"I did. He refused. The Harpers will not be joining us at the reception."

"Not even...?" Byron swallowed, staring out at the mountains cloaked in darkness. "Not even his family? His daughter?"

Suddenly, Matthew understood. "No. Is she the reason you've got a black eye?"

Byron didn't answer. Instead, he said, "Is Whitney Wildz *your* reason?"

"Her name," Matthew said with more force than he probably needed, "is Whitney Maddox. Don't you forget it."

Byron gave him the look—the same look all the brothers shared. The Beaumont smile. "Exactly how 'not available' is she, anyway?"

Deep down, Matthew had to admire how well his little brother was handling himself. In less than a minute, he'd completely redirected the conversation away from Harper's daughter and back to Matthew and Whitney. "Completely not available."

"Well," Phillip announced behind them, "this has been

lovely and dull, but I've got a bride-to-be waiting for me who's a lot more entertaining than you lot."

"And I've got to get home to Serena and Catherine," Chadwick added.

"I swear," Byron said, "I leave for one lousy year and I don't even know you guys anymore. Chadwick, not working? Phillip, sober and monogamous? And you?" He shot Matthew a sidelong glance. "Hooking up with Whitney Wild—"

"Maddox," Matthew corrected.

Byron gave him another Beaumont smile and Matthew realized what he'd just done—tacitly agreed that he was, in fact, hooking up with Whitney. "Right. You hooking up with anyone. Next thing you know, Frances will announce she's joining a nunnery or something."

"We can only hope," Chadwick grumbled before he turned to Phillip and Dale. "You okay to get home?"

Dale spoke. "You're going straight home to the farm?"

"Yeah," Phillip replied, slapping the man on the shoulder. "Jo's waiting on me. Thanks for—"

Matthew cut him off. "I'll see that he gets home."

"What—" Phillip demanded. He sounded pissed.

Matthew didn't look at him. He focused on Dale and Chadwick. "There's been a lot of pressure with this wedding. We can't be too careful."

"—the hell," Phillip finished, giving him a mean look.

Matthew refused to flinch even as he wondered what he was doing. At no point during the wedding planning had Phillip been teetering on the brink of dependency. Why was Matthew implying that he suddenly needed a babysitter?

Because. He wanted to see Whitney.

"Good plan," Chadwick said. "Dale, is that okay with you?"

"Yeah. See you tomorrow at the rehearsal dinner." Dale took off.

When it was just the four brothers, there was a moment of

awkward silence. Then the awkwardness veered into painful. What was Matthew doing? He could see the question on each man's face. Byron's black eye. Casting doubts on Phillip's sobriety. That wasn't who Matthew was. He was the one who did the opposite—who tried to make the family sound better, look better than it really was. He put the family name first. Not his selfish desire to see a woman who was nothing but a PR headache waiting to happen.

Phillip glared at him. Yeah, Matthew had earned that. "Can we go? Or do you need to take a potshot at Chadwick, too?"

Chadwick paused. He'd already headed for the door. "Problem?"

"No. Nothing I can't handle," Matthew hurried to say before Byron and Phillip could tattle on him.

He could handle this. His attraction to Whitney? A minor inconvenience. A totally amazing, mind-blowing inconvenience, but a minor one. He could keep it together. He had to. That was what he did.

Chadwick nodded. That he was taking Matthew at his word was something that should have made Matthew happy. He'd earned that measure of trust the hard way. It was a victory.

But that didn't change the fact that he was, at this exact moment, undermining that trust, as well.

Yeah, he could handle this.

He hoped like hell.

Fourteen

The drive out to the farm was fast and tense.

"After this wedding," Phillip finally said as he fumed in the passenger seat, "you and I are going to have words."

"Fine." Matthew had earned it, he knew.

"I don't get you," Phillip went on, clearly deciding to get those words out of the way now. Matthew thought that it'd be better if they could just fight and get it over with. "If you wanted to come out to the farm and see her, you could have just come. Why'd you have to make it sound like I had my finger on the trigger of a bottle? Because I don't."

"Because."

"What the hell kind of answer is that?"

Matthew could feel Phillip staring at him. He ignored him. Yeah, he'd bent the truth. That was what he did. Besides, he'd covered up for Phillip so many times they'd both lost count.

"You don't have to hide her. Not from us. And certainly not from me. I already know what's going on."

The statement rankled him. The fact that it was the truth? That only made it worse. "I'm not hiding."

"Like hell you're not. What else would you call that little show you put on back there? Why else does Byron have a black eye? You can dress it up as you're protecting her because that's what you do but damn, man. There's nothing wrong with you liking the woman and wanting to spend time with her. You think I'd hold that against you?"

"You would have. In the past."

"Oh, for crying out loud." Phillip actually threw his hands up. "There's your problem right there. You're so damn concerned with what happened last year, five years ago—thirty-five years ago—that you're missing out on the *now*. Things change. People change. I'd have thought that hanging out with Whitney would have shown you that."

Matthew didn't have a comeback to that. He didn't have one to any of it.

Phillip moved in for the kill. Matthew wasn't entirely used to the new, improved, changed Phillip being this right and certainly not right about Matthew. "Even Chadwick would understand if you've got to do something for *you*. You don't have to manage the family's image every single minute of your life. Figure out who you are if you're not a Beaumont."

Matthew let out a bark of laughter. "That's rich, coming from you."

If he wasn't a Beaumont? Not happening. He'd fought too hard to earn his place at the Beaumont table. He wasn't going to toss all that hard work to "figure out" who he was. He already knew.

He was Matthew Beaumont. End of discussion.

"Whatever, man. But the next time you want to cover your tracks, don't use me as a human shield. I don't play these games anymore."

"Fine."

"Good."

The rest of the drive was silent.

Matthew was mad. He was mad at Phillip—but he wasn't sure why. Because the man had spoken what felt uncomfortably like the truth? And Byron—he'd gotten that damn black eye. Because Matthew had asked him to do something dramatic.

And he was—he was mad at Whitney. That was what this little verbal skirmish was about, wasn't it? Whitney Maddox.

Why did she have to be so—so—so *not* Whitney Wildz? Why couldn't she be the kind of self-absorbed celebrity he knew how to manage—that he knew how to keep himself distant from? Why did she have to be someone soft and gentle and—yeah, he was gonna say it—innocent? She shouldn't be so innocent. She should be jaded and hard and bitter. That way he wouldn't be able to love her.

They pulled up at the farmhouse. Matthew didn't want to deal with Phillip anymore. Didn't want to deal with any of it. He was not hiding her, damn it.

He strode into the house as if he owned the thing, which he didn't. Not really. But it was Beaumont Farms and he was a Beaumont, so to hell with it.

He found Jo and Whitney on the sofas, watching what looked like *Rudolph the Red-Nosed Reindeer*, the one he'd watched back when he was a kid. Whitney was already in her pajamas. Jo's ridiculous donkey, Betty, was curled up next to Whitney. She was petting Betty's ears as if it were a normal everyday thing.

Why didn't he feel normal anymore? Why had he let her get close enough to change him?

"Hi," she said in surprise when she looked up. "Is everything—?"

"I need to talk to you." He didn't wait for a response. Hell, he couldn't even wait for her to get up. He scooted Betty out of the way and pulled Whitney to her feet.

"Are you—*whoa*!"

Matthew swept her legs up and, without bothering to look back at where Phillip was no doubt staring daggers at him—hell, to where the donkey was probably staring daggers at him—he carried Whitney up the stairs.

She threw her arms around his neck as he took the steps two at a time. "Are you okay?"

"Fine. Just fine." Even as he said it, he knew it wasn't true. He wasn't fine and she was the reason.

But she was the only way he knew how to make things fine again.

"Bachelor party went okay?" she asked as he kicked open the door to her room.

"Yeah. Fine." He threw her down on the bed and wrenched off his tie.

Her eyes went wide. "Matthew?"

"I—I missed you, okay? I missed you." Why did saying it feel like such a failure? He didn't miss people. He didn't miss women. He didn't let himself care enough to miss them.

But in two damn days, he'd missed her. And it made him feel weak. He wrapped the tie around his knuckles and pulled, letting the bite of silk against his skin pull him back. Pull him away from her.

She clambered up to her knees, which brought her face almost level with his. "I missed you, too."

"You did?"

She nodded. Then she touched his face. "I…I missed waking up with you."

At her touch—soft and gentle and innocent, damn it all—something in him snapped. "I don't want to talk."

She was the reason he was the mess he was. He had to—he didn't know. He had to put her in her place. He *had* to keep himself distanced from her, for his own sanity. And he couldn't do that while she was touching him so sweetly, while she was telling him she missed him.

One eyebrow notched up. Too late, he remembered announcing that the whole reason he was sweeping her off her feet was to talk to her.

But she didn't say anything. Instead, she pushed herself up onto her feet and stripped her pajama top off. Then, still standing on the bed—not tipping over, not accidentally kicking him—she shimmied out of her bottoms, which was fine because it was damnably hard to think the lustful thoughts he was thinking about someone who was wearing pink pants covered with dogs in bow ties. Then she sank back down to her knees in front of him.

No talking. No touching. He would keep a part of himself from her, just as he did with everyone else. No one would know what she meant to him. Not even him.

Then he had her on her back, but that was still too much. He couldn't look into her eyes, pale and wide and waiting for him. He couldn't see what he meant to her. He couldn't risk letting her see what she meant to him. So he rolled her onto her belly and, after getting the condom, buried himself in her.

She didn't say a word, not even when her back arched and her body tightened down on his and she grabbed the headboard as the climax rolled her body. She was silent as he grabbed her hips and drove in deep and hard until he had nothing left to give her.

They fell onto the bed together, panting and slick with sweat. He'd done what he needed to—what a Beaumont would. This was his birthright, wasn't it? White-hot affairs that didn't involve feelings. His father had specialized in them. He'd never cared about anyone.

Matthew needed to get up. He needed to walk away from Whitney. He needed to stay a Beaumont.

Then she rolled, looped her arms over his neck and held him. No words. Just her touch. Just her not letting him go.

How weak was he? He couldn't even pull himself away from her. He let her hold him. Damn it all, he held her back.

It was some time before she spoke. "After the wedding… after Christmas morning…"

He winced. "Yes?" But it was surprisingly hard to sound as if he didn't care when his face was buried in the crook of her neck.

"I mean," she hurried on, her arms tightening around his neck, "that'll be... We'll be..."

It. That'll be it. *We'll be* done. That was what she was trying to say. Then—and only then—did he manage to push himself up. But he couldn't push himself away from her. "My life is here in Denver, and you..." He swallowed, wishing he were stronger. That he could be stronger for her. "You need the sun."

She smiled—he could see her trying—but at the same time, her eyes began to shine and the corners of her mouth pulled down. She was trying not to cry. "Right."

He couldn't watch her, not like this. So he buried his face back against her neck.

"Right," he agreed. *Fine*, he thought, knowing it wasn't. At least that would be clean. At least there wouldn't be a scene that he'd have to contain. He should have been relieved.

"Anytime you want to ride the Trakehners," she managed to get out, "you just let me know."

Then—just because she made him so weak—he kissed her. Because no matter how hard he tried, he couldn't hold himself back. Not around her.

Fifteen

They spent the next morning looking over the carriage that would pull Phillip and Jo from the chapel to the reception. The whole thing was bedecked with ribbons and bows of red-and-green velvet, which stood out against the deep gray paint of the carriage. Whitney wasn't sure she'd ever really grasped what the word *bedecked* meant, but after seeing the Beaumont carriage, she understood completely. "It's a beautiful rig."

"You like it?" Matthew said. He'd been quiet all morning, but he'd held her hand as they walked around the farm together. In fact, he had hardly stopped touching her since they'd woken up. His foot had been rubbing against her calf during their breakfast; his hands had been around her waist or on her shoulders whenever possible.

Whitney had been worried after last night. Okay, more than worried. She'd originally thought that he was mad at her because of the picture with Frances, but there'd been something else going on.

After the intense sex—and the part where he'd agreed that this relationship was short-term—she had decided that it wasn't her place to figure out what that "something else" was. If he wanted to tell her, he would. She would make no other claims to him.

She would try not to, anyway.

"I do." She looked at the carriage, well and truly bedecked. "It's going to look amazing. And with Jo's dress? *Wow.*"

He trailed his hand down her arm. She leaned into his touch. "Do you have a carriage like this?"

She grinned at him. He really didn't know a whole lot about horses, but he was trying. For her. "Trakehners aren't team horses, so no."

He brushed his gloved fingertips over her cheek. She could feel the heat of his touch despite the fabric. "Want to go for a ride?"

She pulled up short. "What?"

"I'll have Richard hook up the team. Someone can drive us around."

"But…it's for the wedding."

"I know. You're here *now.*" Then he was off, hunting up a hired hand to take them on a carriage ride around Beaumont Farms.

Now. Now was all they had. Matthew gallantly handed her up into the carriage and tucked the red-and-green-plaid blankets around her, then wrapped his arm around her shoulder and pulled her into him. Then they were off, riding over the snow-covered hills of the farm. It was…magical.

She tried not to overthink what was happening between them—or, more to the point, what wasn't going to happen in a few days. What was the point of dwelling on how she was going to go back to her solitary existence, with only her animals and crazy Don to break up the monotony?

This was what she wanted—a brief, hot Christmas-vacation romance with a gorgeous, talented man. A man who would make her feel as if Whitney Maddox was a woman who didn't have to hide anymore, who could take lovers and have relationships. This was getting her out of the safety of her rut.

This time with Matthew was a gift, plain and simple. She couldn't have dreamed up a better man, a better time. He was, for lack of a better word, *perfect*.

That had to be why she clung to him extra hard as they rode over the ice-kissed hills, the trees shimmering under the winter sun. This was, hands down, the most romantic thing she'd ever done—even though she knew the score. She had him now. She didn't want to miss any of that.

So when it was time to go to the rehearsal, she went early with Matthew. They were supposed to eat lunch, but they wound up at his palatial apartment, tangled up in the sheets of his massive bed, and missed lunch entirely. Which was fine. She could eat when she was alone. And the dinner after the rehearsal would be five-star, Matthew promised.

They made it to the chapel for the rehearsal almost an hour ahead of everyone else—of course they did. The place was stunning. The pews were decorated with red-and-gray bows that matched the ones on the carriage perfectly atop pine garlands, making the whole place smell like a Christmas tree. The light ceilings had dark buttresses and the walls were lined with stained-glass windows.

"We're going to have spotlights outside the windows so the lights shine at dark," Matthew explained. "The rest of the ceremony will be candlelit."

"Wow," Whitney breathed as she studied the chapel. "How many people will be here for the wedding?"

"Two hundred," he said. "But it's still an intimate space. I've been working with the videographers to make sure they don't overtake the space. We don't want anything to distract from the happy couple."

She took a deep breath as she held an imaginary bouquet in front of her. "I should practice, then," she said as she took measured steps down the aisle. "Should have brought my shoes."

Matthew skirted around her and hurried to the altar. Then he waited for her. Her cheeks flushed warm as an image of her doing this not in a dove-gray gown but a long white one forced its way across her mind.

Now, she thought, trying not to get ahead of herself. *Stay in the now.*

That got harder to do when she made it up to the altar, where Matthew was waiting. He took her hands in his and, looking down into her eyes, he smiled. Just a simple curve of the lips. It wasn't rakish; it wasn't predatory—heavens, it wasn't even overtly sexual.

"Ms. Maddox," he said in a voice that was as close to reverent as she'd ever heard him use.

"Mr. Beaumont," she replied because it seemed like the thing to do. Because she couldn't come up with anything else, not when his gaze was deepening in its intensity.

It was almost as if, standing here with Matthew, in this holy place…

No. She would not hope, no matter how intense his gaze was, no matter how much his smile, his touch affected her. She would not hope, because it was pointless. She had three more days before she left for California. Tonight, Christmas Eve and maybe Christmas morning. That was it. No point in thinking about something a little more permanent with him.

He leaned forward. "Whitney…"

Say something, she thought. *Something to give me hope.*

"Hello? Matthew?"

To his credit, he didn't drop Whitney's hands. He did lean back and tuck her fingers into the crook of his arm. "Here," he called down the aisle as the wedding planner came through the doors. Then, to Whitney, he said, "Shall we practice a few times before everyone gets here?"

"Yes, let's." Which were not words of hope.

That was fine. She didn't want any.

Really.

* * *

Against his will, Matthew sent Whitney home with Jo and took Phillip back to his place. Even though they were going to shoot photos before the ceremony, Jo had decided that she wanted to at least get ready without Phillip in the house.

Phillip wasn't exactly talking to Matthew, which was fine. Matthew had things to do anyway. The press was lining up, and Matthew had to make sure he was available for them before they wandered off and started sniffing around.

This was his job, his place in this world. He had to present the very best side of the Beaumonts, contain any scandals before they did real damage and…

His mind drifted back to the carriage ride across the farm with Whitney—to the way she'd looked standing hand in hand with him at the altar.

For such a short time, it hadn't mattered. Not the wedding, not the public image—not even the soft launch of Percheron Drafts. His showroom-ready apartment, his fancy cars—none of that mattered.

What had mattered was holding a beautiful woman tight and knowing that she was there for him. Not for the family name, the fortune, the things.

Just him.

And now that time was over and he was back to managing the message. The good news was that Byron's little brawl had done exactly what Matthew had intended it to—no one was asking about Whitney Wildz.

He checked the social media sites again. Whitney had insisted on keeping her hat on during the rehearsal and the following dinner and had only talked with the embedded press representatives when absolutely required. He knew he should be thankful that she was keeping her profile as low as possible, but he hated that she felt as if she had to hide.

All was as calm as could be expected. As far as he could tell, no one in attendance had connected the quiet maid of honor with Whitney Wildz. Plus, the sudden influx of famous people eating in restaurants and partying at clubs was good press, reinforcing how valuable the Beaumont name was without Matthew being directly responsible for their actions.

It wouldn't last, he knew. He sent out the final instructions to the photographer and videographer, which was semipointless. Whitney was in the wedding party, after all. And he hadn't let her change her hair. They'd have to take pictures of her. But reminding the people on his payroll what he expected made him feel better anyway.

They just had to get through the wedding. Whitney had to make it up the aisle and back down without incident.

Just as she'd done today. She'd been downright cute, miming the action in a sweater and jeans and that hat, of course. But tomorrow?

Tomorrow she'd be in a gown, polished and proper and befitting a Beaumont wedding. Tomorrow she'd look perfect.

He could take a few days after the wedding, couldn't he? Even just two days off. This thing had swallowed his life for the past few months. He'd earned some time. Once he got Phillip and Jo safely off on their honeymoon and his siblings and stepmothers back to their respective corners, once he had Christmas dinner with his mom, he could…

He could go see Whitney. See her in the sun. Ride her horses and meet her weird-looking dogs and her pop-singer cats.

This didn't change things, he told himself as he began to rearrange his schedule. This was not the beginning of something else, something *more*. Far from it. They'd agreed that after the wedding, they were…done.

Except the word felt wrong. Matthew had never had a problem walking away from his lady friends before. When it was over, it was over. There were no regrets, no looking back and absolutely no taking time off to spend a long weekend together.

It was close to midnight when he found himself sending her a text. What are you doing? But even as he hit Send, he knew he was being foolish. She was probably in bed. He was probably waking her up. But he couldn't help himself. It'd been a long day, longer without her. He just wanted... Well, he just wanted her.

A minute later, his phone pinged and there was a blurry photo of Whitney with a tiny donkey in her lap. He could just see the silly dogs in bow ties on her pajama pants. Jo had leaned over to grin into the frame, but there was no missing Whitney's big smile. Watching *Love Actually* and eating popcorn, came the reply.

Good. Great. She was keeping a low profile and having fun at the same time.

Then his phone pinged again.

Miss you.

He could take a couple of days. Maybe a week. Chadwick would understand. As long as they made it through the wedding with no big scandals—as long as all the Beaumonts stayed out of the news while he was gone—he could spend the time with Whitney.

Miss you, too, he wrote back. Because he did.

He was pretty sure he'd never missed anyone else in his life.

The day of the wedding flew by in a blur. Manicures, pedicures, hairstylists, makeup artists—they all attacked Whitney and the rest of the wedding party with the efficiency of a long-planned military campaign. Whitney couldn't tell if that was because Matthew had everything on a second-by-second schedule or if this was just what happened when you had the best of the best working for you.

She finally met Byron Beaumont, as he was next in the makeup artist's chair after they finished painting Whitney's lips scarlet-red. She winced as she looked at the bruise around his face that was settling into purples and blues like a sunset with an attitude.

"Ms. Maddox," he said with an almost formal bow. But he didn't touch her and he certainly didn't hug her, not as Frances had. Heck, he didn't even call her Whitney Wildz. "It's an honor."

"I'm sorry about your eye," she heard herself say, as if she were personally responsible for the bruising. Byron looked a great deal like Matthew. Maybe a few inches shorter, and his eyes were lighter, almost gray. Byron's hair was almost the same deep auburn color as Matthew's, but his hair was longer with a wave to it.

Byron grinned at her then—almost the exact same grin that Matthew had and that Phillip had. "Anything in the service of a lady," he replied as he settled into the chair, as if he had his makeup done all the time.

By four that afternoon, the ladies were nibbling on fruit slices with the greatest of care to sustain them through the rest of the evening. "We don't want anyone to pass out," the wedding planner said as she stuck straws into water bottles and passed them around.

Then they were at the chapel, posing for an endless series of photos. She stood next to Jo, then next to Frances, then between Frances and Serena. They took shots with Jo's parents, her grandmother, her aunt and uncle. Since Toni Beaumont was singing a song during the wedding, they had to have every permutation of who stood where with her, too.

Then the doors to the chapel opened, and Whitney heard Matthew say, "We're here." The men strode down the aisle as if they owned the joint. At first she couldn't see them clearly. The chapel wasn't well lit and the sunlight streaming in behind them was almost blinding. But then, suddenly, Matthew was leading the Beaumont men down the aisle.

She gasped at them. At him. His tuxedo was exquisitely cut. He could have been walking a red carpet, for all the confidence and sensuality he exuded.

"We're keeping to the schedule, right, people?" he demanded. Then their gazes met and the rest of the world—the stylists and wedding planner chatting, the photographer bossing people around—all of it fell away.

"Perfect," he said.

"You, too," she murmured. Beside her, Frances snickered. Oh, right—they weren't alone. Half the Beaumont family was watching them. She dropped her gaze to her bouquet, which was suddenly very interesting.

Matthew turned his attention to the larger crowd. "Phillip's ready for the reveal."

"Everyone out," the photographer announced. "I want to get the bride and groom seeing each other for the first time. Joey," he said to Jo. He'd been calling her that for half an hour now. Whitney was pretty sure it wouldn't be much longer before Jo cracked and beat the man senseless with his own camera. "You go back around and walk down the aisle."

Jo glanced at Whitney and rolled her eyes, which made them both giggle. Whitney gathered up Jo's train, and they hurried down the aisle as fast as they could in these dresses. It was only when they had themselves tucked away that Frances gave the all clear.

Whitney and Frances peeked as Jo made her way up the aisle to where Phillip was waiting for his bride. "I don't know if I've ever seen him that happy," Frances whispered as Phillip blinked tears of joy out of his eyes. "I hope it lasts."

"I think it will," Whitney decided.

"I just…" Frances sighed. "I just wish we could all stop

living in our father's shadow, you know? I wish I could be-lieve in love. Even if it's just for them."

"Your time will come," Whitney whispered as she looked at Frances. "If you want it to."

"I don't. I'm never getting married," Frances announced. Then, standing up straighter, she added, "But if you want to marry Matthew, can I be your bridesmaid?"

Whitney opened her mouth and then closed it because as much as she wanted to tell Frances her head was in the clouds and that after tonight Whitney and Matthew were going their separate ways, she couldn't dismiss the image of him stand-ing with her at the very same altar where Jo and Phillip now stood. For that brief moment—when she'd wanted him to say something that would give her hope that they weren't done after this. When she'd thought he was going to do just that. And then they'd been interrupted.

Finally, she got her mouth to work. "I'm not going to marry Matthew."

"Pity," Frances sniffed. "I saw how he looked at you. Trust me, Matthew doesn't look at other people like that."

So everyone had seen that look. Whitney sighed. But before she could respond, a deep voice behind them said, "Like what?"

The women spun around at Matthew's voice. Whitney teetered in her shoes, but Matthew caught her before she could tip forward. Then his arms were around her waist, and he was almost holding her. But not quite. They managed to keep a glimmer of space between them.

"Hi," Whitney breathed. She wanted to tell him how much she'd missed him. She wanted to ask if they could spend this last night together, after the reception, so that their Christmas morning could start off right. She wanted to tell him that he was the most handsome man she'd ever seen.

She didn't get the chance.

"Like that," Frances said with obvious glee.

"Frannie." Matthew's voice was as clear a warning as Whitney had heard since that very first night, when he'd realized who she'd once been. The space between him and Whitney widened ever so slightly. "Go make sure Byron stays out of trouble, please."

Frances rolled her eyes. "Fine. I'm going, I'm going. But he's not the one I'm worried about right now." Then, with a rustle of silk, she was gone.

And they were alone in the vestibule. "You look amazing," she managed to get out.

"So do you," he said as his arms tightened around her.

"I'd kiss you, but…"

"Lipstick," he agreed. "We're going to have to go out for more photos soon."

A quick moment. That was all they had. But she wanted more. She at least wanted tonight. One more night in his arms. Then, somehow, she'd find a way to let him go. "Matthew…" she said.

At the same time, he said, "Whitney…"

They paused, then laughed. But before she could ask for what she wanted, the photographer called out, "The best man and maid of honor? Where are you, people?"

"Tonight," Matthew said as he looped his arm through hers. "We'll talk at the reception, all right?"

All she could do was nod as they walked down the aisle together, toward the happy couple and the bossy photographer.

Whitney didn't trip.

Sixteen

Everything went according to plan. After they finished the photos in the chapel—including a series of shots with Betty in her flower-girl-slash-ring-bearer harness—the whole party went to a nearby park and took shots with snow-covered trees and ground as the backdrop. They also did the shots of Jo and Phillip getting into and out of the carriage.

Then, just because everything was going so smoothly, Matthew asked the photographer to take pictures of each of the couples with the carriage, just so he and Whitney could have a photo of the two of them with the Percheron team. So they'd have something to remember this week by.

Serena and Chadwick didn't mind, but Frances and Byron clearly thought he was nuts and Matthew didn't miss the look Phillip gave him.

He wasn't hiding how he felt about Whitney, okay? He *wasn't*. That wasn't why he had the photographer take extra shots of all the couples by themselves. He reasoned that Chadwick and Serena had had a small ceremony—absolutely no pomp and circumstance had been allowed. True, Serena had been about seven months pregnant and, yes, Chadwick had already had a big wedding for his first marriage. Serena's parents had walked her down the aisle while Phillip,

Matthew and Frances stood as witnesses. Cell phone photos didn't count. So Matthew was really doing this for Chadwick and Serena, so they'd have beautiful photos of them at their very best. And if Matthew and Whitney got some memories out of it, so much the better.

And because he was not hiding how he felt about her, he had his arms on her while the photographer snapped away. An arm around her waist when they leaned underneath the evergreen tree, its branches heavy with glistening snow. Handing her up into the carriage. Tucking her against his waist.

For their part, his family was…okay with it. Byron had slapped him on the back and said, "Some women are worth the bruises, huh?" Matthew had ignored his baby brother.

Chadwick's big comment was, "The situation is under control, correct?"

To which Matthew had replied, "Correct." Because it was. For the moment, anyway.

"You doing okay?" Matthew whispered to Phillip as they stood at the front of the chapel. He could see that Phillip had started to fidget.

"Why is everything going so slow?" Phillip whispered back as Frances did the "step, pause, step, pause" walk down the aisle to Pachelbel's *Canon in D.* "I want Jo."

"Suck it up and smile. Remember, the cameras are rolling."

Matthew looked out over the full house in the chapel. Phillip's mother had a place of honor in the front, although she had chosen not to sit with Jo's family. Which didn't surprise Matthew a bit. Eliza Beaumont was not a huge fan of anything that had to do with the Beaumont family, a list that started with Matthew and went on for miles.

But Phillip had wanted his mother at his wedding and Matthew had the means to make it happen, so the woman was sitting in the front row, looking as relaxed as a prisoner before a firing squad and pointedly ignoring everyone.

Serena was headed down the aisle now, although she was moving at a slightly faster clip than Frances had been. "Beautiful," Chadwick whispered from the other side of Matthew. "I have to say, I'm impressed you pulled this off."

"Don't jinx it, man," Matthew hissed through his smile.

Then Serena was standing next to Frances and everyone waited.

Matthew could see Whitney, standing just inside the doors. *Come on, babe,* he thought. *One foot in front of the other. You can do it. It'll be fine.*

Then the music swelled and she took the first step. Paused. Second step. Paused. Each foot hit the ground squarely. She didn't wobble and she didn't trip on her hem. She *glided* down the aisle as if she'd been born with a bouquet in her hand and a smile on her face. The whole time, she kept her gaze fastened on him. As though she was walking not just to him but *for* him.

God, she was *so* beautiful. Simply perfect. But then, the woman in her doggy pajamas had been perfect, too. Even when she was klutzy and nervous and totally, completely Whitney, she was absolutely perfect.

How was he going to let her go?

She reached the altar and took her place. He could see how pleased she was with herself, and frankly, he was pretty damn happy, too.

Then there was a moment that should have been silent as the music changed to the wedding march and Jo made her big entrance.

Except it wasn't silent. A murmur ran through the crowd—the highest of Denver's high society, musicians and actors and people who were famous merely for being famous.

Then he heard it. "…Whitney Wildz?" Which was followed by "…that hair!" More murmurs followed. Then a click. The click of a cell phone snapping a picture.

He looked at Whitney. She was still smiling, but it wasn't

the same natural, luminous thing it'd been earlier. Her face was frozen in something that was a mockery of joy.

It'll be okay, he wanted to tell her. He wanted to believe it.

Then the music swelled up, drowning out the whispers and the clicks. Everyone stood and turned to the entrance. Betty tottered down the aisle as the daughter of one of the brewery's employees tossed rose petals onto the ground. Betty should have held everyone's attention.

But she didn't. Not even a mini donkey wearing a basket and a crown of flowers over her floppy ears could distract from Whitney Wildz. People were holding their devices high to get the best shot of her.

Jo came down the aisle on the arms of her parents. Matthew took advantage of this to get the wedding rings untied from the small pillow on Betty's back, and then the farm manager, Richard—looking hilariously uncomfortable in a suit—led the small animal off before she started munching on the floral arrangements.

When he stood back up, Matthew caught Whitney's eye as Jo took her place at the altar. He gave her an encouraging nod, hoping that she'd get the message. *Ignore them. Don't let them win.*

When the music stopped this time, the murmuring was even louder. The preacher took his place before the happy couple. Jo handed Whitney her bouquet.

The murmuring was getting louder. People weren't even trying to whisper now. Matthew wanted to shout at the crowd, *This is a wedding, for God's sake! Have some decency!* But he'd long since learned that you didn't feed the fire like that. Ignoring the excited whispers was the only way to make it through this.

"*Matthew,*" Chadwick said in the quietest of whispers, and Matthew knew what his older brother was thinking. This was having the situation under control? *This* was handling it?

The preacher began to talk about vows and love, but he had to stop and pitch his voice up in volume to be heard.

Matthew kept his attention on the happy couple—and on Whitney. She was blinking too fast, but her smile was locked. Her face looked as if it were going to crack in half. She didn't look at him, but she didn't need to. He could read her well enough.

This was just like the restaurant all over again. She'd done nothing—not even tripped, much less fallen, and yet she was setting off a media firestorm. He had the sinking feeling that if he got out his phone and checked social media, Whitney would already be trending.

Then, out of the corner of his eye, he saw it. Movement, in the aisle. As best he could without turning and staring, he looked.

Oh, hell. People were getting up and exiting the pews—coming into the aisles. Phones and cameras were raised. They were jostling—yes, jostling—for a better shot. Of Whitney. Of someone they thought was Whitney Wildz.

"If I may," the preacher said in a tone better suited for a fire-and-brimstone Sunday sermon than a Christmas Eve wedding. "If I may have *silence*, please."

That was when Whitney turned her stricken face to his. He saw the tears gathering, saw how fast she was breathing. "I'm sorry," she said, although he couldn't hear her over the crowd. He read her lips, though. That was enough.

"No," he said, but she didn't hear him. She was already turning to hand Jo's bouquet to Serena and then she was running down the aisle, arms stiffly at her side.

Gone.

Oh, hell.

"Ms. Maddox?"

Whitney realized that she was outside.

The horse-drawn carriage was parked in front of the cha-

pel, waiting for the happy couple. The happy couple whose
wedding she'd just ruined. She vaguely recognized the driver
as one of the farmhands, but he wasn't wearing jeans and
flannel. "Is everything okay?"

"Um…" No. Nothing was okay. And worse? She didn't
know when it would start being okay again. The chapel was
on a college campus. She had to walk…that way to get to
a main road?

Snow began to fall on her bare shoulders. She hadn't even
managed to snag her cape, but who cared. She wasn't going
back in there. She was going…

Home. That was where she was headed. Back to her solitary ranch where she could live out her solitary life. That was
where she belonged. Where she wouldn't embarrass herself,
which was bad enough. She was used to that.

She'd ruined Jo's wedding. Her best friend—hell, her only
friend—and Whitney had ruined the wedding. She hadn't
fallen, hadn't even dropped her bouquet.

She'd just been herself.

Why had she ever thought she could do that?

She wrapped her arms around her waist to try and keep
warm as she walked away from the carriage and the driver.
She didn't really have a plan at this point, but she knew she
couldn't take off in the wedding carriage. The very carriage
she'd ridden in yesterday, snuggled in Matthew's arms. She'd
already messed up the wedding. She drew the line at steal-
ing the carriage.

"Ms. Maddox?" the driver called behind her, but she ignored him. She needed to get back to the farm so she could
get her things and go—and there was no way the horse and
carriage could get her there.

She'd walk to the main road and catch a taxi. Taxis could
get her to the farm and from there, she could leave. There.
That was a plan.

The snow was coming down thick and fast, each flake

biting into her bare shoulders with what felt like teeth. It felt as if it were trying to punish her, which was fine. She deserved it.

She'd tried. She'd tried *so* hard. She'd offered to step aside. She'd tried to convince Matthew to let her change her hair. And she damn well had on panties today. Industrial-strength Spanx in opaque black, just to be extra sure.

But it wasn't enough. It would never be enough. She would *always* be Whitney Wildz. And every time she got it into her foolish little head that she wasn't—that she could be whoever she wanted to be—well, this was what would happen. If she didn't hurt herself, she'd hurt the people she cared for. People like Jo.

People like Matthew.

God, she couldn't even think of him without pain. She'd *told* him she was going to ruin the wedding, but the man had decided that through the sheer force of his will alone, she wouldn't. He'd been bound and determined—literally—to have the perfect Beaumont wedding. He was a man who was used to getting what he wanted. He'd given her a chance to show him—to show everyone—that she was Whitney Maddox. For a beautiful moment—a too-short moment—she'd thought they had succeeded.

But that'd been just an illusion and they were both the poorer for indulging in it. He had to hate her now. She was living proof that he couldn't control everything. He'd never be able to look at her and see anything but imperfection.

She slipped but managed not to fall. The sidewalks were getting slicker by the second and these shoes weren't suited for anything other than plush carpeting. She could hear the sounds of traffic getting closer, and she trudged on. Good. The farther she could get from the wedding, the better.

Her stomach turned again. She hoped Jo and Phillip were still *able* to get married. What if the whole thing had devolved into a brawl or something? What if the preacher decided Whitney's running was a sign from God that Jo and Phillip shouldn't be married? It was on her head. All of it.

She'd just come upon the main street when she heard "Whitney?" from behind her.

Matthew. No, God, please—not him. She couldn't look at him and see his failure and know it was hers.

She waved her hands, hoping there was a taxi somewhere. Anywhere. And if there wasn't, she'd keep walking until she found one.

"Whitney, wait! Babe," she heard him shout. Damn it, he was getting closer.

She tried to hurry, but her foot slipped. Stupid heels on the stupid snow. The whole universe was out to get her. She thought she would keep her balance but she hit another slick spot and started to fall. Of course. Maybe someone would get a picture of it. It'd make a great headline.

Instead of falling, though, she was in his arms. The warmth of his body pushed back against the biting cold as he held her tight. It was everything she wanted and nothing she deserved. "Let me go," she said, shoving against him.

"Babe," he said, pointedly not releasing her from his grip. If anything, he held on tighter. "You're going to freeze. You don't even have your cape."

"What does it matter, Matthew? I ruined the wedding. You saw how it was. You and I both knew it was going to happen and…and we let it." The tears she'd been trying not to cry since the first whisper had hit her ears threatened to move up again. "Why did I let it happen?"

He came around to her front and forced her to look at him. He was not gentle about it. "Because you're Whitney Maddox, damn it. And I don't care about Whitney Wildz. You're enough for me."

"But I'm not and we both know it. I'm not even enough for me. I can never be the perfect woman you need. I can never be perfect." The tears stung at her eyes almost as much as the snow stung against her skin. And that, more than anything else, hurt the most.

"You *are*," he said with more force. "And you didn't ruin the wedding. Those people—they did. This is on them. Not you."

She shook her head, but before she could deny it—because Matthew had never been more wrong in his life—shouts of "Whitney? Whitney!" began to filter through the snow.

A taxi pulled up next to them and the cabbie shouted, "You need a cab, lady?"

Matthew got a fierce look on his face. "Let me handle them," he said as he stripped off his tuxedo jacket and wrapped it around her shoulders. "Follow my lead. I can fix this."

She wanted to believe it. She wanted him to protect her, to save her from herself.

But she couldn't. She couldn't let him throw away everything he'd worked for because of her. She wasn't worth it.

"Don't you see? I can't be another mess you have to clean up. I just can't." She ducked under his arm and managed to get the taxi door open on the second try. "It has to be this way," she told him.

Before the press could swarm, she got in the taxi and slammed the door. Matthew stood there, looking as if she'd stabbed him somewhere important. It hurt to look, so she focused on the cabbie.

"Where to, lady?" he asked.

"Can you take me to the Beaumont Farms? Outside the city?"

The cabbie stared at her dress, then at Matthew and the press, complete with flashing cameras and shouting. "You can pay?"

"Yes."

The fare would be huge, but what did it matter?

This evening had already cost her everything else.

Seventeen

Matthew was going to punch something. Someone. Several someones.

Hard.

Whitney's taxi sped off, its wheels spinning for traction on the newly slick streets. Then the press—the press *he* had invited to the wedding—was upon him like hungry dogs fighting over the last table scrap.

"Matthew, tell us about Whitney!"

"Matthew! Did you see Whitney Wildz drinking before the wedding? Can you confirm that Whitney Wildz was drunk?"

"Was she on drugs?"

"Is there something going on, Matthew? Are you involved with Whitney Wildz?"

"Did Whitney have a baby bump, Matthew? Who's the father?"

"Is Byron the father? Is that why he has a black eye? Did you two fight over her?"

The snow picked up speed, driving into his face. It felt good, the pain. It distracted him from the gut-wrenching agony of Whitney's face right before she ran down the aisle. Right before she got into the taxi.

"Ladies and gentlemen," he said in his meanest sneer. There were no such people before him. Just dogs with cameras.

No one blinked. The sarcasm was lost on them entirely. They just crowded closer, microphones in his face, cameras rolling. For a moment, he felt as if he were back in college and, at any second, someone was going to ask him what he thought about those photos of his father with his pants around his ankles.

Panic clawed at him. No one had ever asked if he wanted to manage the Beaumont public image. It was just something he'd fallen into and, because he was good at it, he'd stuck with it. Because it earned him a place in the family. Because defending his father, his brothers, his stepmothers—that was what made him a Beaumont.

Figure out who you are if you're not a Beaumont.

Phillip's comment came back to Matthew, insidious little words that Matthew had thought were Phillip's attempt at chipping away at Matthew's hard-won privilege.

But if being a Beaumont meant he had to throw Whitney to the dogs…could he do that? Did he want to?

No. That was not what he wanted. It'd never been, he realized. Hadn't he asked Byron to generate some press? Hadn't that been putting Whitney first?

Who am I? Her voice whispered in his ear. *Who am I to you?*

She'd said those words to him in the front seat of his car, right before he'd tied her to the bed.

She was Whitney Maddox. And she was Whitney Wildz. She was both at the same time.

Just as he was Matthew Beaumont and Matthew Billings. He'd never stopped being Matthew Billings. That lost little boy had always been standing right behind Matthew, threatening to make him a nobody again.

Because if he wasn't a Beaumont, who was he? He'd always thought the answer was a nobody. But now?

Who was *he* to *her*?

Who was he?

He was Matthew Beaumont. And being a Beaumont was saying to hell with what people thought of you—to hell with even what your family thought of you. It was not giving a rat's ass what the media said.

Being a Beaumont was about doing what you wanted, whenever you wanted to do it. Wasn't that what was behind all of those scandals he'd swept under the rug for all these years? No one else in his family ever stopped to think. They just *did*. Whatever—whoever—they wanted.

He looked at the cameras still rolling, the reporters all jostling for position to hear what juicy gossip he was going to come up with. The headlines tomorrow would be vicious—but for the first time in his life, he didn't care.

"Ladies and gentlemen," he began again, "I have no comment."

Dead silence. Matthew smirked. He'd truly managed to stun the lot of them into silence.

Then he turned and hailed a cab. Mercifully, one pulled right up to the curb.

"Where to, buddy?" the cabbie asked as Matthew shut the door on the gaping faces of the press.

Who was he? What did he want?

Whitney.

He had to get her. "The Beaumont Farms, south of the city."

The cab driver whistled. "That's gonna cost you."

"Doesn't matter." Then, with a smile, he added, "I'm a Beaumont."

Eighteen

"Ms. Maddox?" The guard stepped out of the gate when Whitney climbed out of the taxi. "Is everything all right?"

She really wished people would stop asking that question. Wasn't the answer obvious? "I…I need to pay him and I don't have any money. On me. I have some cash in the house…" She shivered. The cabbie had turned the heat on full blast for her, but it hadn't helped. Matthew's jacket wasn't enough to fend off the elements. The snow was coming down thick and fast and the cabbie was none too happy about the prospect of making it home in this weather.

The guard stared at her with obvious concern. Then he ushered her into the guard house. "I'll pay the driver and then get a truck and take you to the house. Don't move."

He said it as if he was afraid she might go somewhere, but she didn't want to. There was heat in this little building.

Plus, she was almost back to the farmhouse. This nice guard would take her the rest of the way. She'd get out of this dress and back into her own clothes. She didn't have much. She could be packed within twenty minutes. And then…

If she left immediately, she could be home by tomorrow afternoon. Back to the warmth and the sun and her animals and crazy Donald, none of whom would ever care that she'd ruined the Beaumont Christmas wedding. Yes. Back to the safety of solitude.

The guard came back with a truck and helped her into the passenger seat. He didn't tell her how much it had cost to get the cabbie to drive away. She'd pay it back, of course. She'd use the money from the royalty checks for *Whitney Wildz Sings Christmas, Yo*. Fitting.

"I'm going home," she told him when he pulled up in front of the house and got out to unlock the front door for her. "Tonight."

"Ms. Maddox, the snow is going to continue for some time," he said, the worry in his voice obvious. "I don't think—"

"I can drive on snow," she lied. She couldn't stay here. That much she knew.

"But—"

Whitney didn't listen. She said, "Thank you very much," and shut the door in the man's face. Which was a diva thing to do, but it couldn't be helped.

She didn't get lost on her way back to what had been her room and Matthew's room. Their room. Well, it wasn't that anymore.

She changed and started throwing things into her bags. She'd have time when she got home to shake out the wrinkles. She didn't have that time now.

The dress…it lay in a heap on the floor, as if she'd wounded it in the line of duty. She'd felt beautiful in the dress. Matthew had thought so. She'd felt…

She'd felt like the woman she was supposed to be when she'd worn it. Glamorous and confident and sexy and worthy. And not scandalous. Not even a little.

She picked it up, shook it out and laid it on the bed. Then she did the same with his tuxedo jacket. In her mind's eye, she saw the two of them this afternoon, having their pictures taken in a park, in a carriage bedecked in Christmas bows.

They hadn't even gotten to walk down the aisle together. She'd ruined that, too.

Her bags were heavy and, because she hadn't packed carefully, extra bulky. Getting them both out of the door and down the hall was bad enough. She was navigating the stairs one at a time when she heard the front door slam open.

"Whitney?"

Matthew. *Oh, no.* That was all that registered before she lost her grip on one of her bags. It tangled with her feet and suddenly she was falling down the last few stairs.

And right into his arms. He caught her just as he had before—just as he was always doing.

Then, before she could tell him she was sorry or that she was leaving and she'd pay back the cab fare, he was kissing her. His hair was wet and his shirt was wet and he was lifting her up to him, sliding his hands around her waist and holding her.

And he was kissing her. She was so stunned by this that she couldn't do anything but stare at him.

He pulled away, but he didn't let her go. Hell, he didn't even set her on her feet. He just held her as though his life depended on it.

She needed to get out of his arms so she could go back to being invisible Whitney Maddox. But she couldn't. Was it wrong to want just a few more minutes of being someone special? Was it wrong to want that hope, even if she was going to get knocked down for daring to hope almost immediately?

Matthew spoke. "*Always* kiss me back," he said, as if this were just another wild Tuesday night and not the ruination of everything. Then her bags—which had come crashing down after her—seemed to register with him. "Where are you going?"

"Home," she told him. She would not cry. Crying solved

nothing. And really, this was everything she'd expected. "I don't belong here. I never did."

"That's not true."

Oh, so they were just going to deny reality? Fine. She could do that. "Why are *you* here? Why aren't you at the wedding?" Then, because she couldn't help herself—because she might never get another chance to have him in her arms—she placed her palm on his cheek.

He leaned into her touch. "I had this revelation," he said as he touched his forehead to hers. "It turns out that I'm not a very good Beaumont."

"What?" she gasped. She'd heard him say how hard it was to earn his place at the table—at the altar. Why would he say that about himself? "But you're an amazing man— you take care of people and you took your sister and brother to my concert and the whole wedding was *amazing*, right until I ruined it!"

His grin was sad and happy and tired, all at the same time. Her feet touched the ground, but he didn't let her go.

"A Beaumont," he said with quiet conviction, "wouldn't care what anyone else thought. They wouldn't care how it played in the media. A Beaumont would do whatever he wanted, whenever he wanted, consequences be damned. That's what makes a Beaumont. And I've never done that. Not once." He paused, lifting her up even closer. "Not until I met you."

Hope. It was small and felt foreign in her mind—so foreign that she almost didn't recognize it for what it was. "Me?"

"You. For the first time in my life, I did something because I wanted to, regardless of how it'd play in the press." He touched her hair, where the bejeweled clip still held her stubborn white streak in place. "I fell in love with you."

Her heart stopped. Everything stopped. Had he just said… that he'd fallen in love with her? "I—" But she didn't have anything else.

Then, to her horror, she heard herself ask, "Who am I to you?"

He gave her a little grin, as if he'd known she was going to ask the question but had hoped she wouldn't. "You're a kind, thoughtful, intelligent woman who can get clumsy when you're nervous. You'd do anything for your friends, even if it puts you in the line of fire."

"But—"

He lifted her face so she had to look at him. "And," he went on, "you're beautiful and sexy and I can't hold myself back when I'm around you. I can't let you go just because of how it'll look in a headline."

"But the press—tomorrow—" She shuddered. The headlines would be cruel. Possibly the worst in her life, and that was saying something. The Beaumont public image would be in tatters, thanks to her. "Your family... I ruined *everything*," she whispered. Why couldn't he see that?

His grin this time was much less sweet, much more the look of a man who could bend the press to his will. "You merely generated some PR, that's all. And there's no such thing as bad PR."

"That's not— What?"

"Don't let the guessing games that complete strangers play hold you back, Whitney. Don't let a manufactured scandal keep us apart."

"But—but—but your life is here. And I need the sun. You said so yourself."

"The Beaumonts are here," he corrected her. "And we've already established that I'm not a very good Beaumont."

The thing that was hope began to grow inside of her until it was pulsing through her veins, spreading farther with each heartbeat. "What are you saying?"

"Who am I?" His voice was low and serious. It sent a chill up her spine that had nothing to do with his wet shirt. "If I'm not a Beaumont, who am I to you?"

"You're Matthew." He swallowed, his Adam's apple bobbing nervously. "It never mattered to me what your name is—Billings, Beaumont—I don't care. I came here thinking it'd be nice to meet a man who could look at me without thinking about Whitney Wildz or all the headlines. A man who could make me feel sexy and wanted, who could give me the confidence to maybe start dating. Who could show me it was even possible."

He cupped her face in his hands, his thumbs stroking her cheeks. "And?"

"And...that man was you. Eventually," she added with an embarrassed smile, remembering the first time she'd fallen into his arms. "But now the wedding's over. And I—" Her voice caught. "I can't be another mess you have to manage, Matthew. And I can't ever be perfect. You know I can't."

"I know." For the briefest of seconds, it felt like a book being slammed shut. "But," he added, "I don't want perfection. Because I'll never get it. I can try and try to be the perfect Beaumont until I lie down and die and I'll never make it. That's what you've shown me."

A little choked sob escaped her lips. No matter what she did, she'd never be perfect, either. Not even to him. "Great. Glad to help."

"Be *not* perfect with me, Whitney. Let me be a part of your life. Let me catch you when you fall—and hold me up when I stumble."

"But...the press—the headlines—"

"They don't matter. All that matters is what you and I know. And this is what I know. I have never *let* myself fall in love before, because I've been afraid that loving someone else will take something away from me. Make me less of a man, less of a Beaumont. And you make me more than that. More than my name. You make me whole."

The impact of his words hit her hard. Suddenly, those tears that she hadn't allowed herself to cry because the disappointment and shame were always to be expected—suddenly, those tears were spilling down her cheeks. "I didn't expect to find you. I didn't expect to fall in love with you. I don't—I don't know how to do this. I don't want to mess this up. More than I already have."

"You won't," he said, brushing his lips over hers. "And if you try, I'll tie you to the bed." She giggled, and he laughed with her. "We will make this work because I'm not going to let you go. You will always be my Whitney. Although," he added with a wicked grin, "I was thinking—you might want to try out a new last name. Maybe something that starts with a *B*."

"What are you saying?"

"Marry me. Let me be there for you, *with* you."

"Yes. Oh, God—*Matthew*." She threw her arms around his neck. The tears were coming faster now, but she couldn't hold them back. It was messy and not perfect but then, so was life. "You see me as I really am. That's all I ever wanted."

"I *love* you as you really are." He swept her feet out from underneath her and began to climb the stairs back to his room. Their room. "Love me back?"

"Always," she told him. "Always."

* * * * *

If you loved
A BEAUMONT CHRISTMAS WEDDING,
Don't miss the rest of
the BEAUMONT HEIRS *trilogy!*

NOT THE BOSS'S BABY
TEMPTED BY A COWBOY

Available now from Sarah M. Anderson
and Harlequin Desire!

COMING NEXT MONTH FROM

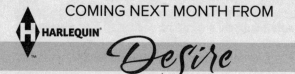

HARLEQUIN®
Desire

Available December 2, 2014

#2341 THE SECRET AFFAIR
The Westmorelands • by Brenda Jackson
Facing her family's disapproval, Jillian ended her affair with
Dr. Aidan Westmoreland. But he knows their passion won't be
denied—not for secrets or mistakes. And he'll follow her around
the world to prove it...

#2342 PREGNANT BY THE TEXAN
Texas Cattleman's Club: After the Storm • by Sara Orwig
When Stella discovers she's pregnant from one passionate night with
Aaron, she declines his dutiful marriage proposal. But the Dallas mogul
lost one family already; he doesn't intend to lose this child—or Stella!

#2343 THE MISSING HEIR
Billionaires and Babies • by Barbara Dunlop
When tragedy struck, Amber took care of Cole's infant half brother. Yet a
custody battle soon forces Cole to claim the child...and lie to the woman
he can't seem to resist. Will he ever win Amber's trust?

#2344 CHRISTMAS IN THE BILLIONAIRE'S BED
The Kavanaghs of Silver Glen • by Janice Maynard
English beauty Emma broke Aidan Kavanagh's heart a decade ago.
Now she's back—as a guest at his brother's Christmas wedding! Will
the truth about her betrayal heal old wounds, or will she lose Aidan
all over again?

#2345 SCANDALOUSLY EXPECTING HIS CHILD
The Billionaires of Black Castle • by Olivia Gates
Reclaiming his heritage means everything to Raiden Kuroshiro, until his
passion for Scarlett Delacroix threatens all of his plans...and her life. Will
he give up everything he thought he wanted to keep her and his baby?

#2346 HER UNFORGETTABLE ROYAL LOVER
Duchess Diaries • by Merline Lovelace
Undercover agent Dominic St. Sebastian learns he's technically a royal
duke. But when the woman who discovered his heritage is attacked,
leaving her with amnesia, it seems the only person the bewildered
beauty remembers is him... _____

YOU CAN FIND MORE INFORMATION ON UPCOMING HARLEQUIN® TITLES,
FREE EXCERPTS AND MORE AT WWW.HARLEQUIN.COM.

HDCNM1114

REQUEST YOUR FREE BOOKS!
2 FREE NOVELS PLUS 2 FREE GIFTS!

HARLEQUIN® *Desire*

ALWAYS POWERFUL, PASSIONATE AND PROVOCATIVE

YES! Please send me 2 FREE Harlequin Desire® novels and my 2 FREE gifts (gifts are worth about $10). After receiving them, if I don't wish to receive any more books, I can return the shipping statement marked "cancel." If I don't cancel, I will receive 6 brand-new novels every month and be billed just $4.55 per book in the U.S. or $4.99 per book in Canada. That's a savings of at least 13% off the cover price! It's quite a bargain! Shipping and handling is just 50¢ per book in the U.S. and 75¢ per book in Canada.* I understand that accepting the 2 free books and gifts places me under no obligation to buy anything. I can always return a shipment and cancel at any time. Even if I never buy another book, the two free books and gifts are mine to keep forever.

225/326 HDN F4ZC

Name _____ (PLEASE PRINT) _____

Address _____ Apt. # _____

City _____ State/Prov. _____ Zip/Postal Code _____

Signature (if under 18, a parent or guardian must sign)

Mail to the **Harlequin® Reader Service:**
IN U.S.A.: P.O. Box 1867, Buffalo, NY 14240-1867
IN CANADA: P.O. Box 609, Fort Erie, Ontario L2A 5X3

Want to try two free books from another line?
Call 1-800-873-8635 or visit www.ReaderService.com.

* Terms and prices subject to change without notice. Prices do not include applicable taxes. Sales tax applicable in N.Y. Canadian residents will be charged applicable taxes. Offer not valid in Quebec. This offer is limited to one order per household. Not valid for current subscribers to Harlequin Desire books. All orders subject to credit approval. Credit or debit balances in a customer's account(s) may be offset by any other outstanding balance owed by or to the customer. Please allow 4 to 6 weeks for delivery. Offer available while quantities last.

Your Privacy—The Harlequin® Reader Service is committed to protecting your privacy. Our Privacy Policy is available online at www.ReaderService.com or upon request from the Harlequin Reader Service.

We make a portion of our mailing list available to reputable third parties that offer products we believe may interest you. If you prefer that we not exchange your name with third parties, or if you wish to clarify or modify your communication preferences, please visit us at www.ReaderService.com/consumerschoice or write to us at Harlequin Reader Service Preference Service, P.O. Box 9062, Buffalo, NY 14269. Include your complete name and address.

HD13R

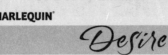
Here's a sneak peek of
THE SECRET AFFAIR
by New York Times *and* USA TODAY *bestselling author*
Brenda Jackson

Dr. Aidan Westmoreland entered his apartment and re-moved his lab coat. After running a hand down his face, he glanced at his watch, frustrated. He'd hoped he would have heard something by now. What if…

The ringing of his cell phone made him pause. It was the call he'd been waiting for. "Paige?"

"Yes, it's me."

"Is Jillian still going?" he asked, not wasting time with chitchat.

There was a slight pause on the other end, and in that short space of time knots formed in his stomach. "Yes, she's still going on the cruise, Aidan."

He released the breath he'd been holding as Paige con-tinued, "Jill still has no idea I'm aware that the two of you had an affair."

Aidan hadn't known Paige knew the truth either, until she'd paid him a surprise visit last month. According to her, she'd figured things out the year Jillian had entered medical school. She'd become suspicious when he'd come home for his cousin Riley's wedding and she'd overheard him call Jillian Jilly in an intimate tone. Paige had been concerned this past year when she'd noticed

Jillian seemed troubled by something that she wouldn't share with Paige.

Paige had talked to Ivy, Jillian's best friend, who'd also been concerned about Jillian. Ivy had shared everything about the situation with Paige. Which had prompted Paige to fly to Charlotte and confront him. Until then, Aidan had been clueless as to the real reason behind his and Jillian's breakup.

When Paige had told him about the cruise she and Jillian had planned and she'd suggested an idea for getting Jillian on the cruise alone, he'd readily embraced it.

"I've done my part and the rest is up to you, Aidan. I hope you can convince Jill of the truth."

Moments later he ended the call and continued to the kitchen, where he grabbed a beer. Two weeks on the open seas with Jillian would be interesting. But he intended to make it more than just interesting. He aimed to make it productive.

A determined smile spread across his lips. By the time the cruise ended there would be no doubt in Jillian's mind that he was the only man for her.

*Find out how this secret affair began—and how
Aidan plans to claim his woman in
THE SECRET AFFAIR by New York Times and
USA TODAY bestselling author Brenda Jackson.*

*Available December 2014,
wherever Harlequin® Desire books and ebooks are sold!*

HARLEQUIN®

Desire

ALWAYS POWERFUL, PASSIONATE AND PROVOCATIVE.

USA TODAY bestselling author
Sara Orwig

Brings you the next installment of
Texas Cattleman's Club: After the Storm

PREGNANT BY THE TEXAN

Available December 2014

When folks think of Stella Daniels, they think unassuming, even plain. But after a devastating tornado hits Royal, Texas, Stella steps up and leads the recovery effort. That's when she attracts the attention of construction magnate Aaron Nichols—and a surprising night of passion ensues.

Aaron sees something special in the no-nonsense admin, and he's more than happy to bring her out of her shell. But when he discovers Stella's expecting his child, can he overcome his demons to be the hero this hometown heroine really needs?

Don't miss other exciting titles from the
Texas Cattleman's Club: After the Storm:

STRANDED WITH THE RANCHER
by Janice Maynard

SHELTERED BY THE MILLIONAIRE
by Catherine Mann

Available wherever books and ebooks are sold.

HD733552